WITCHING WITH SHARKS

A WITCH ON THE ROCKS COZY MYSTERY
BOOK FOUR

LILY HARPER HART

HARPERHART PUBLICATIONS

ONE

"Come here." Grayson "Gray" Hunter's voice was husky as he leaned into the opening of the tiki bar and attempted to draw Hali Waverly closer to him. They'd officially been dating two weeks now, but if he was being honest—even with himself—he would admit it felt as if they'd been destined for each other since before then.

He didn't say that out loud, though. At least not yet. He didn't want to appear schmaltzy in front of his sarcastic witch. He felt it though. He often wondered if she did as well.

"I'm working." Hali shot Gray a flirty smile before sliding through the back door of her tiki bar at Paradise Lodge Golf Course and Resort and delivering a tray of drinks to a table on the patio. Gray watched her, his heart expanding when she smiled and chatted away with her patrons, and then he kept his eyes on her when she returned.

He thought she would slide back into the tiki hut and continue working. Instead, she approached him and pressed herself to his back, allowing her lips to drift close to his ear.

"If you're a good boy, I'll reward you later," she promised in a low voice.

Gray swore his eyes crossed at the images she was conjuring, but he managed a smile in return as she shot him a knowing look on her way back to the tiki hut to make more drinks. "I'm going to hold you to that," he warned.

"Knock yourself out," she called back.

When Gray looked to his right, he found the stalwart Annabelle Hutchinson watching him with overt disdain.

"What?" he demanded defensively.

"You guys are gross," Annabelle replied, not missing a beat. "It's like you're in heat or something."

It was a charge Gray couldn't deny. Under different circumstances, he might be embarrassed about the way he was acting. The thing is, he honestly didn't care what others thought about him. Especially where Hali was concerned. She made him feel ... lighter. That was the best word he could come up with to describe his new outlook on life. He had no intention of stopping the flirting because that also made him happy. And, if the smile Hali was shooting him now was to be believed, she was happy too. That's what he wanted for her more than anything.

"You could always not look," Gray argued as he sipped his beer. He was spending the night at Hali's place on the resort grounds, so he wasn't worried about imbibing too much. He wasn't the type to lose control and accidentally tie one on, however. He didn't even really care about the beer. He just wanted to be with Hali, even if she had to work.

"Oh, look at you." Annabelle often vacillated between serious and snarky. Gray knew Hali liked the woman and allowed her to conduct business from the bar because they'd built up a friendship. That's why he merely sat back on his stool and waited for her to finish it out. "You're just a smitten kitten, aren't you?"

Gray's eyebrows winged up, and he practically choked on

a laugh. "I don't believe I'm comfortable with that term," he said finally, amused despite himself.

"What term would you prefer?" Ever practical, Annabelle got right to the heart of matters.

"What are my options?"

"You could be cupcakin'," she offered.

Gray frowned. "I have no idea what that means, but I'm certain we're not doing it." He looked to Hali for confirmation and almost got lost in her eyes. "Right?"

Hali's lips quirked. "I don't think I can say I'm cupcakin' ... whatever that is," she agreed.

"Fine." Annabelle wasn't about to be denied, so she cocked her head. "You could be smorny."

Gray didn't have to ask what that was. "No." He vehemently shook his head. "I am not smorny." He seemed to take a moment to consider it after the fact. "Well, wait ... I might be smorny, but I can't use that word."

Hali laughed as she went to the blender to mix another drink. She was doing that more often now, Gray noted. Laughing so loudly it warmed up the very atmosphere around her. She wasn't an unhappy person before they hooked up, but she was always on guard against appearing weak. Now she was like a starfish, unfurled and open, and he swore he was falling harder and harder for her with each passing day.

How had that even happened? He didn't have an answer, but he wasn't about to run from what he was feeling either. At one time, he might've done just that. She made him feel content, though, and the turmoil that had chased him his entire life was no longer at the forefront of his brain. He liked the contentment so much he didn't care if he had to tell people he was smorny to keep it.

"I think you're definitely smorny," Hali whispered as she gave him a quick kiss before swinging out of the tiki bar with another load of drinks.

Gray watched her go, his heart growing in his chest. Then he noticed the way she was favoring her right hip, and his stomach sank. He was an alpha guy—sort of literally—and he'd tried pushing her for hip surgery to ease some of the pain she was constantly feeling. She wasn't ready yet, however, and that frustrated him to no end.

Because he knew she needed a break and would never admit it, he swung his attention to Kendra, one of Hali's workers. The tiki bar was doing a solid business tonight. It wasn't, however, overflowing. That was yet to come because the resort wasn't expecting an influx of guests until the following day. That meant Hali could take a break tonight.

"Can you handle the bar for fifteen minutes?" he asked Kendra in a low voice.

Kendra slid her eyes to him, seemingly confused, and then she glanced at Hali. "She's doing that thing where she leans against the palm tree to hide the fact that her hip hurts," she noted.

Gray nodded. "I'm going to carry her out to the beach for fifteen minutes and rub that hip. She won't let me do it in front of people. That will leave you alone though."

Kendra smirked. "Is it just the hip you're going to rub?"

Gray made a face. "For now. I don't like seeing her in pain."

Kendra let loose a heavy sigh. "I get it. I was just joking. Take her away for a bit. I can handle the bar."

Gray shot her a grateful look and then waited for Hali to return to the tiki bar. He didn't miss the grimace she tried to hide from him when she dropped the tray on the counter, but there was no hiding the "eek" she emitted when Gray's arm slid around her waist and he lifted her from the ground.

"What are you doing?" she demanded, her cheeks flushing with color.

"We're taking a break together." Gray's tone was firm, a warning that he was willing to fight about this.

"I'm fine," she argued, likely knowing full well what he was doing.

Because he couldn't stand the thought of even an ounce of discomfort knocking her down—he could not sit on that stool and watch her grit it out, which was her norm—Gray opted for a different tack. "I need a few minutes with you alone, or I might explode," he pleaded.

Hali's expression was hard to read. Was she buying it? Probably not. Ultimately, she nodded, however, and that told Gray her hip was hurting more than usual. Rather than snap at her and make demands about a surgery she was terrified to undergo, he placated himself when she rested her head against his shoulder and allowed him to carry her out to a cabana.

"Oh, this is nice," Hali murmured as Gray situated them on one of the loungers, positioning her between his legs and allowing her to rest her back against his chest. Even though he wanted to play flirty games, Gray instead started rubbing her hip and tried not to react when she erupted in the sort of moan he'd only ever heard under different circumstances.

"That's quite the noise there, baby," he teased when she did it again.

A laugh escaped as Hali closed her eyes and let him work his magic. "Sorry."

"Don't ever apologize for making that noise," Gray said solemnly as he studied the water, his eyes narrowing when he thought he caught a hint of something that shouldn't have been there. "That's my favorite sound in the world."

"You just got distracted," Hali noted, drawing his eyes down to her. "What did you see?" She looked resigned, even ready to face some action.

"Nothing to worry about," Gray assured her, leaning in for a soft kiss. "The only thing you have to worry about for the next fifteen minutes is me doing this." He dug his fingers into her hip and grinned when she practically screeched in delight. "People are going to think I'm killing you in here if you're not careful," he warned.

"I don't care. That feels so good, I don't care what they think we're doing."

"I don't either." Gray kept rubbing and then went back to staring at the water. His eyesight was better than most—it came from his shifter heritage—and he was certain he'd seen a fin in the water this time when he scanned. It wasn't a dolphin fin either.

"Okay, this time I know you saw something," Hali pressed. "What's wrong? I don't want you hiding something from me because you think I'm fragile."

"That is the exact opposite of what I'm doing," Gray said gravely, forcing his eyes to her. "It's just ... there's a shark in the water."

Hali immediately started shaking her head. "There's a shark net."

"Occasionally, sharks get through the shark net," Gray pointed out. "I don't think that's what we're dealing with though."

Hali's forehead creased, and he recognized the exact moment she grasped what he was getting at. "Shark shifters?" She almost looked excited at the prospect. "I've only ever seen a handful of them. They're supposed to be rare."

Gray scowled. "I'm a shark shifter."

"I've never seen you shift into a shark."

"That's because I can't do it." Gray was embarrassed to admit it. He was dual natured—wolf and shark—but he'd only ever been able to embrace the wolf. He knew Hali would be thrilled to see the shark, but there was nothing he could do to make it happen. He'd tried. More than once.

As if reading his mind, Hali turned earnest. "You're perfect the way you are, however that is."

A smile took over Gray's features as he regarded her. "You're perfect the way you are too."

"Which is why you had to swoop in and carry me away to rest for fifteen minutes." Hali's smile slipped. "I'm sorry about that."

"Oh, Hali, don't." Gray shook his head. He knew she felt bad about her hip. She was constantly apologizing when they had to rest during a walk, or when she almost tripped because her hip wasn't ready for her full weight in the morning. He hated it. "We'll talk about the surgery when you're ready. You don't have to push yourself."

"Even though your life would be easier if I just shut up and got it?" Hali teased.

"I don't need my life easier. I just want you. When you're ready, you'll know it."

"Yeah." Hali exhaled heavily and closed her eyes. "Keep rubbing."

Gray smirked. "And here I thought you would be more excited about seeing a potential shark shifter coming out of the Gulf," he teased.

"Oh, I totally want to look if that's the case, but it doesn't appear our friend is coming in," she replied. "At least not right now."

"Yeah." Gray rested his cheek on top of her head, his fingers busy as he rubbed her. It didn't take him long to find the fin again. The shifter—he was convinced that's what they were dealing with—showed no signs of hitting the beach. For now, he would have to wait it out. "I wonder what he or she is doing here."

"It's probably the trivia competition," Hali replied. She was practically purring thanks to Gray's deft fingers. "That's taking over the beach this weekend."

"Oh, right." Gray had forgotten about the trivia competition, even though there were signs all over the resort. It was easier for him to stay with Hali at Paradise Lodge than it was for them to travel across town to stay at his place ... although they had done that when having a night out on the town together. "What's the deal with the trivia competition again?"

"It's being hosted by the Wentworth Group," she explained. "They're the ones responsible for that new Daze Beer brand."

"Oh, the ones who name their beers things like Hallucination, and Galactic Frappe Phantasm," Gray replied on a grimace.

"That would be them," Hali agreed, grinning. "I guess the trivia competition is supposed to be a big deal. The final purse is five hundred grand."

Gray jolted. "That's quite the reward. For trivia?"

His incredulous expression made Hali laugh. "I felt the same way. It's a big deal though. You know Lana? The regular who comes to my bar every other day?"

Gray didn't have to search his memory to conjure an image of the woman in question's face. She was unforgettable. "You mean Fun Fact Girl," he replied.

Hali doused him with a quelling look. "She's a wonderful person."

"I didn't say she wasn't. She's simply the reason I know that the Gulf of Mexico encompasses around 617,800 square miles of water and that male babies are often born with erections because penises are literally born ready."

Hali snorted so hard she almost choked, which had Gray grinning down at her.

"She really is a good person," Hali insisted when she'd managed to curtail her laughter. "She's just... I think she might be on the spectrum. She doesn't read a room well."

Gray brushed her hair away from her face. "I like Lana

fine," he promised. He meant it. "She just drops fun facts at weird times. If she's participating in the trivia game, more power to her." His eyes drifted back to the water, to where the shark fin continued to cut back and forth. "I think she's going to have her hands full with the competition though."

"It's a big purse," Hali agreed shifting a bit so he could have easier access to her hip. "I think, from our perspective, that could mean big trouble."

Gray wasn't surprised by the observation. If Lana couldn't read a room, Hali more than made up for it. She was better at reading people than anybody he had ever met. "I was just thinking that," he acknowledged. "We'll likely have paranormals crawling out of the woodwork to come and claim that big prize."

"Most paranormals are fine," she reminded him.

"Most," he agreed, his eyes on the fin.

"You're still worried," Hali surmised. She'd only known Gray for a few months at this point, but she could read him well. Gray thought he would hate that familiarity. He'd been wrong. He loved it.

"I don't know if 'worried' is the word I would use," he hedged. "I just want you to be careful. If this place is going to be overwhelmed with paranormals, it's always best to watch your back."

"Aren't you going to be watching my back? I mean, that is what you do when I'm serving drinks at the bar. You watch my back and make suggestive comments."

Because he was amused, Gray squeezed her butt while grinning. "I do enjoy watching your back. This is different though." He didn't want to frighten her, but he figured being aware of her surroundings would serve as a benefit regardless. "If the shark shifters are here—and I have to think we have at least one of them out there patrolling the waters right now—that means they'll be focused on that prize."

"I like shark shifters," Hali argued. "They're cool."

"You haven't really spent time with shark shifters."

"I've spent time with you." Hali was adamant. "I like you."

Warmth suffused Gray's chest as he looked down at her. "I like you too." He kissed the tip of her nose. It was more than like. It was more than lust. It was way too early to say love, but he wasn't entirely certain his heart had gotten the memo. From the first moment he'd crossed paths with her, he'd felt something profound. He couldn't explain it, but she stirred emotions in him he'd thought long since dormant. Neither of them were ready for the big L-bomb just yet though. He would have to bide his time.

"You really look worried," Hali said after several seconds of studying him. "What do you think is going to happen?"

"I don't know." Gray opted for honesty. "I just know something *is* going to happen. I can't explain it."

"I get it." Hali bobbed her head. "I get feelings too. You can't stop living your life because of a feeling though. If there's going to be trouble, we'll find that out soon enough. Don't let it ruin your night."

"Does that mean you want me to keep rubbing you?" Gray's eyes twinkled.

"Absolutely. Also, if you're really worried, you can just stay with me at my place all week while the trivia competition is happening. That means you won't miss anything."

When Gray glanced down at her, he found she wasn't looking at him. He didn't miss the tinge of pink on her cheeks as she plucked at invisible lint on her shorts. She wasn't good about opening herself up emotionally. The simple statement had been a leap from her, and he would never slap back her hand when she extended it in his direction.

"That sounds good to me. There's nothing I love more than waking up next to you." She giggled when he tickled her.

"I'll probably have to run home long enough to grab more clothes though. I can do that tomorrow after breakfast, before the festivities start."

"Yeah." Hali let loose a sigh, as if she'd been holding her breath. "So, you'll be here all week. That's good."

Gray could've pushed her on the subject, teased her to within an inch of her life. He didn't, however. He wanted her to be comfortable making these offers going forward. "It's definitely good." When he looked toward the water again, the fin was gone. "There's nowhere I'd rather be than with you."

"I feel exactly the same way," Hali said softly.

"That's convenient, huh?"

"I was thinking the exact same thing."

Two

Living in a warm climate meant the AC ran twenty-four-seven in Hali's villa. She was used to it, and often found herself cocooned in three blankets when she woke in the morning. Since Gray was a hot sleeper—it was the wolf in his blood—that had changed since they'd regularly started spending their nights together. She woke up warm every day now, and it was something she relished.

"What are you thinking?" Gray murmured the next morning when Hali started to stir. His eyes were still closed, but there was a content smile on his face.

"I was thinking that you're like my own personal heating blanket," Hali replied as she snuggled close to him. "I was also thinking that we have only spent one night apart since that first night we spent together."

It was embarrassing for her to talk about this stuff. She wasn't known for being overly effusive. Gray's easygoing nature when it came to matters of the heart made it easier for her to give voice to what she was feeling, however, and she was thankful for it.

"Ah, you're referring to that fourth night, when we both

thought it was best to at least pretend we weren't just going to fall into a serious relationship right out of the gate," Gray mused. "Yes. That was a lonely night. Let's not do that again." He buried his face in her hair. "I'm fine admitting we're already in a serious relationship."

That right there was one of the things Hali liked most about Gray. He didn't hold back. It was as if he knew exactly what she was thinking and wanted to encourage her at every turn. "I'm fine with it too," she realized out loud. "It kind of feels like it was always leading to this."

"It does feel that way," he agreed. "There's no sense slowing things down when we're happy at warp speed."

Hali lifted her head, a wide smile stretching across her features. "You're such a geek," she said on a laugh.

"I did fancy myself Captain Kirk when I was a kid."

"Did you dress up like him for Halloween?" Hali found she wanted to know everything there was to know about Gray. Even the mundane things felt important.

"I grew up in a pack," he reminded her. His hair was messy from sleep, as was hers, but he didn't care. They both loved their mornings together. "We didn't really celebrate Halloween."

Hali was horrified. "You didn't go trick-or-treating?"

He shook his head.

"You didn't dress up?"

He shook his head again.

"You didn't watch horror movies and make yourself sick on Kit Kats before bed?"

"I don't think I have to ask your opinion on this subject," he said on a laugh.

"That just blows," Hali complained. "I love Halloween."

"Well, I know it's a few months away, but maybe you can teach me how to do Halloween right this year."

Hali's eyes sparked as she grinned down at him. "Can I pick out a costume for you?"

Gray opened his mouth to respond and then snapped it shut. He seemed to be rethinking his initial response. "Within reason," he replied after several seconds of contemplation. "I get veto power. You can't dress me up as anything weird."

"You could be Captain Kirk."

"Would you dress up like Uhura?"

"I don't know. I'll have to think about it. I was considering dressing up like a mermaid this year. I saw this really great coconut bra."

Gray made a sputtering sound. "I take it back. Go with your initial plan."

She laughed, as he'd likely intended. "We'll see. As you said, it's months away." She ran her hand over his bare chest. "I like that I can make plans with you that are still months out and you don't act weird about it," she admitted in a low voice.

"Why would I act weird about it?"

She shrugged. "Some guys feel as if they're being boxed in by a woman if she tries to make them commit to something so far down the road."

"Well, I'm not that guy. I want to commit." He paused for a second. "Actually I'm already committed. I don't care how far down the road you want to make plans for. I'll be there."

And because she believed that Hali's insides relaxed a little bit. "How about we just commit to breakfast for this morning?" she suggested after several seconds. "I'm starving. I also want to hear if there's any gossip about the trivia contest before everybody starts arriving. Mindy over at the breakfast place always has the best gossip."

"That sounds good to me." Gray wrapped his arms around her waist and drew her flush with his chest before she could escape. "Ten more minutes of this, and then we'll head out. I want to commit to that too."

Hali smiled as she let him enfold her in his arms. "That sounds like a great idea."

"I was hoping you would like it."

THEY SHOWERED, CHANGED INTO SIMPLE SHORTS and T-shirts, and then headed toward the restaurant. Gray watched Hali carefully to see how she was moving without letting on what he was doing. He was grateful that she didn't appear to be walking with a limp or fighting off stiffness, but he knew from past experience that the hip pain grew throughout the day. She seemed fine for now, so his smile was at the ready when they entered the dining room.

Hali had explained to him upon their first breakfast at the restaurant that the reason such a prime location was only open in the mornings was because they ran the room service from the same location during the afternoons and at night. Gray was a big fan of the restaurant because it was never busy when they visited. That meant they could have a quiet breakfast without having to deal with a bunch of resort visitors.

"Hey, girlfriend," Mindy Grant called out when she saw them. "Take a seat. You guys both want coffee and your regular juice?"

Hali nodded and only released Gray's hand when they were sitting across from one another at the table. "I'm starving," she announced. "I could eat ten breakfasts right now, I swear."

"If you want to eat ten breakfasts, then I want you to eat ten breakfasts," Gray replied easily.

"I think I'll just start with one and see how I feel after that."

"Good plan." Gray didn't bother studying the menu. He and Hali had been eating at the restaurant regularly for the past two weeks, to the point where he felt he knew Mindy relatively well. He liked her, and she always had gossip for Hali. Even he found the gossip entertaining despite the fact that he didn't always know the employees they were kibitzing about.

"Anything good?" Hali asked when Mindy returned after putting in their breakfast orders. There was nobody else in the restaurant at this point, so they could gossip at will.

"Well, you know Chris down at the cabanas, right?" Mindy started.

"Cabana Chris," Hali confirmed on a head bob, not missing a beat. "Does he still have that cold sore problem?"

Mindy snorted, her grin stretching across her face when Gray straightened in his chair. "He *does* have that cold sore problem. He also has a penis problem." She glanced at Gray. "You might want to cover your ears."

"Why would I do that?" Gray demanded as he placed his feet on either side of Hali's under the table. Any physical contact with her was good contact as far as he was concerned.

"Isn't it like lice?" Mindy asked blankly. "Like ... when dudes hear something bad happened to other dudes' penises, they act like it's catching, right? It's just like when hearing about lice and people automatically start scratching their heads."

"I don't think it's like that for me," Gray replied. "If I change my mind, I'll let you know."

"Good man." Mindy winked at him before turning her attention back to Hali. "Apparently, he has some sort of weird mole down there, and he claims it's magical." She lowered her voice to a conspiratorial whisper. "Only problem is, it turns out it wasn't a mole at all. He's just not good at scrubbing his junk, and people are saying it's a tick of some sort."

Hali's mouth dropped open in horror. "Like ... crabs?"

"That's the rumor. Apparently, there's some mutant form of crab out there that eats penises though. It's like a flesh-eating crab." She darted her eyes to Gray, who was indeed shifting on his chair. "Do you wish you'd covered your ears?"

"Unfortunately, yes," Gray replied. "Now I'm going to have nightmares."

"We can wash the sheets later," Hali teased. "Just in case."

Gray glowered at her and then rolled his eyes toward the door of the restaurant. There was movement there—he expected to see one of the other servers or a room service delivery person—but instead he found Cecily Strong strolling through the door.

"Oh, man," he complained when he saw the woman. "This is going to be bad."

Hali followed his gaze. Unlike Gray, she didn't have a negative reaction when seeing Cecily. Of course, that could've been because Cecily was the reason she owned her own bar on the grounds of a very popular tourist destination. When Cecily's boss, Franklin Craven, ran Hali over with a golf cart while drunk—thus causing her hip problems—Cecily swooped in to keep her boss out of jail and helped get Hali a fair deal in trade. The two women were tight now.

"If you're here to ruin our breakfast, you can go someplace else," Gray muttered on a glower. It wasn't Cecily that he disliked, although he did question her common sense at times. It was Franklin he couldn't stand, and not just because the man had once been his uncle and treated his aunt horribly.

"Oh, you're always such a welcoming soul," Cecily teased, ignoring his growl as she sat at one of the open chairs. "I'll have some coffee and avocado toast," she said to Mindy.

"Absolutely." Mindy looked happy to make her escape because Cecily terrified half of the workers on sight. "I'll go put that order in right now."

Cecily waited until she was gone to glance between Hali and Gray. "You two look loved up," she said in her droll tone.

"Jealous?" Gray demanded.

"I just think it's cute." Cecily smirked, but the smile didn't last long. "So, I'm here for a specific reason."

Gray didn't miss the way Hali stiffened. "Don't drag it out," he ordered. "You'd better not be trying to screw Hali. If you are, I'll dig up so much dirt on Franklin—half of which I already have—that he'll lose everything when I make it public." Gray had no idea if it was an effective threat. All that mattered to him was that he was willing to follow through.

"Oh, listen to you," Cecily muttered, shaking her head. "Could you be more of a baby? I have no interest in hurting Hali. Believe it or not, I like her a great deal."

Gray could believe it. There was nothing about Hali that wasn't to be liked. That didn't mean he trusted Cecily. She often had good intentions. Unfortunately for her, the same couldn't be said for Franklin.

"Just be forewarned," he said evenly.

"I'm actually here for you," Cecily countered, smug satisfaction lighting in her eyes when Gray's shoulders jerked in surprise. "Franklin has a job he wants to offer you."

"I am not working for that man," Gray shot back. "I will die first."

"Besides, Gray already has a job," Hali pointed out. "He owns his own private investigation firm."

"This would not be a permanent job," Cecily replied. "It would be more like us hiring Gray's firm to do a job for us."

Even though he hated Franklin with every fiber of his being, Gray found he was intrigued by the conversational shift. "What sort of job?"

"Do you know who Dominic Lawson is?"

Gray's eyebrows moved together in concentration. "I'm not ... wait!" He snapped his fingers. "He's a cupid."

"He is," Cecily readily agreed. "He's high on air magic and all that crap. He does motivational speeches."

"Why is he coming here?" Hali asked. "I think I've heard whispers about him, but I don't know a lot of specifics."

"He's coming for the trivia tournament," Cecily replied, a muscle working in her jaw. "He fancies himself a trivia champion."

"Well, that doesn't seem fair," Hali argued. "He's got air magic."

"Yes, but he argues that's not mind magic," Cecily replied. "The thing is, he can't get near the trivia people anyway. They're buried underneath some sort of magical shield. I asked because I was confused as well. They swear there's nothing he can do to get a gander at the answers."

"That doesn't mean he can't see the answers in the other contestants' heads," Hali pointed out. "He could read their minds and answer before they get a chance."

"I hadn't considered that," Cecily admitted. "I'll have to ask around. Wards could be erected to stop that from happening, though, right?"

"In theory," Hali replied. "I guess."

"In fact, you could do it."

Gray watched as Hali's cheeks flamed pink. "Don't put her on the spot," he admonished Cecily. "You're the ones who decided to have this event and invite paranormals willy-nilly. I believe that means it's up to you to secure your own magical wards."

Cecily shot him a dirty look. "You have the personality of a sour lemon sometimes. Has anybody ever told you that?"

Gray didn't look bothered by the statement. To save Hali, however, he opted to redirect the conversation back to Dominic. "Why does your little cupid celebrity need security?"

"Because women throw themselves on him like he's a pumpkin spice latte in the fall," Cecily replied, not missing a beat. "He attracts women left and right—whether married or unmarried—and it becomes a problem."

Realization dawned on Gray. "And you don't want angry husbands showing up to kill your prized contestant," he surmised.

"In a nutshell," Cecily conceded. "Listen, I get that this might not be your cup of tea—"

"I'll do it." The words were out of Gray's mouth before he could think otherwise.

Surprised, Hali leaned forward. "What do you mean you're going to do it?"

"I'm going to do it," Gray replied easily. "Why not? I'm between jobs right now."

"Yeah, but you hate Franklin." Hali refused to back down. "Why would you want to help him?"

"Why *would* you want to help him?" Cecily echoed. "I hadn't even got to the part where we were going to double your regular fee yet. I figured that's what it would take to get you on our side."

"Oh, you're doubling my regular fee," Gray replied. "I also want one of those armbands you give VIPs that means I can eat and drink wherever I want for free while I'm on the premises. I'm not paying five bucks for a bottle of water."

"That can be arranged." Ever shrewd, Cecily didn't move her narrowed eyes from Gray's face. "You still haven't told me why you agreed so easily, and it's not because you're between jobs." She chewed on her bottom lip thoughtfully for several seconds and then slid her eyes to Hali. "You're not in trouble or anything, are you?"

"Not last time I checked," Hali replied. "He took the job for me though." She was under no delusions otherwise. "Last night, we saw what appeared to be a shark shifter in the water just offshore. He's convinced we're going to see a lot of new paranormals on the scene for this trivia competition."

"I don't disagree," Cecily said. "I think we're going to see a lot of them, and not all of them will be on the up and up. That's another reason I want Gray on the job. Dominic has a very loyal following. He'll bring in a lot of fans. He's strong competition, and I can see certain individuals wanting to take him out of the running because the purse is so big."

"Then I guess it's good that I'll be part of the team," Gray replied. "Just for the record, I am not following orders from Franklin. I draw the line there."

"Yeah, I wouldn't get your hopes up on that one," Cecily said. "Franklin is uptight about this event. He doesn't like Dominic—keeps calling him the little maggot—but he knows he's important for a successful tournament. He's going to be up your butt on this one."

Gray blinked several times and tried to avoid Hali's questioning gaze. After a few seconds, he made eye contact with his beautiful witch and then sighed. "I want triple my usual rate if I'm going to have to put up with Franklin."

Cecily nodded without hesitation. "You've got it."

"And I also want a succession contract for Hali," he added out of the blue.

"What?" Hali sat up straighter. "What are you talking about?"

"A few weeks ago, Franklin was a suspect in a murder, and it became apparent that Hali's deal for the Salty Cauldron wouldn't stick if new ownership came in," Gray persisted. "I want that hole plugged."

Instead of balking, Cecily smirked. "I've already had a contract drawn up. I was trying to figure out how to get Franklin to sign it. I think you just gave me the opening I was looking for."

"I want her protected at all costs." Gray was adamant. "If you can manage that, then I'll deal with Franklin without killing him."

"I think you have yourself a deal." Cecily hopped to her feet. "I'll have the contract here within the hour."

"Thank you." Gray was all smiles as she left.

Hali, however, was dumbfounded. "You didn't have to do that for me," she argued. "You could've gotten something else for yourself."

"Baby, a win for you *is* a win for me. I want you to feel safe more than I want anything else."

Hali blinked hard, telling him she was fighting off tears, and then rested her hand on top of his. "Do you want to take a run back to the villa when we're done here? You know, just to ... um ... spend quality time together?"

Amusement flashed hot on Gray's face. "You read my mind."

"I love that we're so in sync."

"It does feel like a Gulf Coast miracle, doesn't it?"

"And then some."

THREE

Gray gave Hali a heady kiss and promised to check in later at the tiki bar as he reluctantly left the villa after their quick interlude. Cecily met him in the lobby, a smirk prominently fixed on her face.

"What?" he demanded when she crossed her arms over her chest.

"Nothing," she replied in singsong fashion. "I'm just ... marveling at the change in you."

"And what change is that?"

"You're smiling."

"So?"

"So, you've always been a surly beast. Ever since I've known you, which has been a long time. Now you're happy and practically floating. Should I thank Hali for this change in your attitude?"

"Don't give me grief," he warned. "Also, don't give Hali grief. I'm trying to lull her into all-encompassing happiness, so she gets that hip surgery she needs. I don't need you messing it up."

Cecily's smile disappeared. "Yes, well, we both want that."

Her distress was evident. "I happen to like Hali a great deal. I don't want her in constant pain any more than you do."

"She's just scared," Gray replied. He might not have known Hali for a long time, but their bond ran deep. "The surgery is the only option, but if it doesn't work..." He trailed off.

"Then she'll have nothing to hold on to," Cecily surmised.

"Except magic." Gray surprised himself when he said it out loud. "Can she fix herself with magic?"

Cecily held out her hands and shrugged. "I'm not sure. That's out of my realm of expertise."

"Maybe I'll ask her grandmother."

"I would have to think, if the coven had the power to fix Hali's hip, they would've done it already."

"There are other paranormal beings out there," Gray mused, more to himself than Cecily. "I'll do some research. If she doesn't want to have the surgery, it's possible there are other options."

Anything is possible," Cecily readily agreed. "Here is the contract." She produced a folder. "Franklin has signed it. You need to get Hali to sign it in front of a notary and then get it back to me. She'll be protected no matter what under this document."

Gray happily took it. "Thank you."

"You don't have to thank me." Cecily's expression turned dark. "I should've thought about potential loopholes during the original negotiation. I was flummoxed though. I want Hali protected. I've grown quite fond of her."

"Join the club." Gray's cheeky smile was back. "She's pretty cool."

"Oh, look at you." Cecily let loose a taunting chuckle. "I think it's adorable how you two have found one another. I honestly can't wait to see you as parents."

Gray balked, but only initially. "I think it's a bit soon to be talking about kids," he said when he found his voice.

"And yet you've thought about kids with her, haven't you?"

Gray wasn't a liar but admitting to anything of the sort felt odd. "I happen to adore her a great deal."

"Yeah, that's what I thought." Cecily patted his shoulder. "You'll make a good father, surly as you are. Hali will make a wonderful mother. Are you guys going to take over that villa full-time? Hali has it until she no longer needs it at this point, but I have trouble imagining you guys raising kids on resort grounds."

Now Gray was legitimately thrown. "Don't push things."

"Because you're afraid Hali will freak out?"

"No, because I want time with her before we even start discussing those things. Just ... no." He wagged a finger.

"Fine. Let's head up to meet Dominic. He's in the same penthouse Franklin was staying in when you questioned him a few weeks ago."

"What can you tell me about him?"

They headed toward the elevators.

"You're not going to like him." Cecily wasn't one to mince words. "He's full of himself. He believes every woman who crosses paths with him is destined to fall in love with him."

Something occurred to Gray. "He can make that happen, right?" His mind immediately went to Hali. "He can cause anyone who would naturally be attracted to him to do things out of the norm, can't he?"

"My understanding is that sort of stuff is forbidden," Cecily hedged. "The problem is, I don't trust Dominic to follow the rules. Women fall for him at every stop. I don't believe they would do anything out of the ordinary even if trapped in his thrall, though. I think Hali is safe."

"Oh, Hali *will* be safe." Gray's voice was laced with warning. "I'll make sure of that."

"You do you, big guy." Cecily was all business as she led Gray beyond the secure glass door that led to Dominic's penthouse. "Here's a key." She produced one from her pocket. "That gets you in through that door right there and through the penthouse door." She hesitated. "Don't let him know you have it unless it's an emergency. He's the type to cry about something like that."

Gray pocketed the key. "Got it."

Cecily was prim when knocking on the door. The sound of grumbling on the other side heralded trouble in Gray's opinion, but when the door opened to reveal a smiling blond with blue eyes and a dimple, he tempered his knee-jerk assumption and opted to wait it out.

"There you are, my ravishing beauty." Dominic grabbed Cecily's hand and pressed kisses to her wrist. "I thought you'd forgotten about me. It was hurtful."

To her credit, Cecily didn't yank her hand away or mock him. "I was dealing with your security." She gestured for Gray to follow her inside. "This is Gray Hunter. He will be making sure there aren't any incidents on the beach when the tournament begins."

Dominic gave Gray a long once-over, seemingly trying to get a feel for him. "I see," he said after several seconds. "Well, it's nice to meet you." He extended his hand.

Gray shook it, because it was expected, but with every word uttered, he disliked Dominic all the more. "We need to talk about your history with women," he said in his no-nonsense voice.

Dominic's eyebrows hopped. "I'm not sure what you mean."

"It's been intimated that you leave a path of angry husbands in your wake, and I want to make sure that doesn't happen here." Gray sat down on the couch and turned to pertinent matters. "How about you don't use your powers when you're here? How does that sound?"

"Just because women fall for me on a regular basis, that doesn't mean I need to use my powers to make it happen," Dominic argued. "That's not who I am."

Gray didn't believe him for a second. "This place is going to be crawling with paranormals by the end of the day." He was matter of fact. "I saw a shark shifter in the Gulf last night. I don't think this is going to be the best location for you to pull your nonsense."

Dominic blinked twice and then turned his attention to Cecily. "Yeah, this isn't going to work for me. Have you considered perhaps getting me a female bodyguard?"

"No," Cecily replied, not missing a beat. "That is not a consideration. Gray is one of the only people I trust to handle this particular ... assignment. You're going to need to suck it up."

"But I'm the boss," Dominic argued.

"Oh, no." Cecily shook her head. "You were paid a fee to participate in this trivia contest."

That was news to Gray, but he held it together and didn't question the attorney. He could if it became necessary later. For now, he just wanted to listen like a fly on the wall and form his opinions after the fact.

Dominic pinned Cecily with a warning look. "That's private information."

"Gray is head of your security detail," Cecily shot back. "I warned you when you signed the contract that certain rules would have to be followed. Gray is going to make sure that you stick to your contract."

Gray didn't like the phrasing but couldn't argue with the words. "Perhaps we should get to know one another," he suggested, hoping to ease the tension flowing through the room. "After that, we'll discuss what is and isn't acceptable."

Dominic made a protesting sound. "I'm the boss here. Me."

Gray momentarily pictured Hali's face and any danger Dominic could bring to her. "Yeah, it's not going to play out that way here," he said. "Like I said, though, let's get to know one another, and we'll go from there."

THE TIKI BAR WAS QUIET DURING MORNING hours, and Hali hummed to herself as she wiped down the tables and prepared for the day. Gray's presence in her life had made her a hummer, something she never would've considered before. Now, even though she knew she likely sounded goofy, she couldn't stop herself from delighting in her giddiness.

"You sound a little too happy," a female voice said from the tiki bar, causing Hali to jolt.

When she turned, she found her best friend, Carrie Radish, grinning as she used the beverage gun to fill up a plastic cup. "Help yourself," Hali drawled, shaking her head.

"I don't mind if I do." Carrie filled the cup with her standard lemonade and iced tea and then emerged from the covered bar area. "How's life?"

Hali shrugged. "That feels like a trick question."

"It's not. I'm just making sure things are going well with Gray."

"Things *are* going well." Hali's cheeks burned under her friend's intense scrutiny. "What?" She knew she sounded defensive, but she couldn't seem to stop herself. "What are you thinking?"

"I'm thinking that you're happy, and I'm thrilled," Carrie replied honestly. "Where is Gray? You two have been attached at the hip lately. I didn't think he was leaving your side these days."

"Um, we both have jobs to do," Hali argued. "We're not constantly together."

"That's not what I heard."

"And what did you hear?"

"I heard that Gray carried you out of the tiki bar last night and took you to the beach for a little nookie."

Hali was scandalized. "That's not what happened."

"It is in my head."

Scowling, Hali jabbed a finger at her best friend. "My hip was hurting, and he took me to a cabana for fifteen minutes to rest it. Don't be weird."

"The story I'm picturing in my head is better," Carrie replied. "Don't ruin my fun."

"Whatever." Hali moved back to the table she'd been wiping. "Gray will be hanging around a bit more this week though." She was glad Carrie couldn't see her face because she couldn't stop smiling. "He's going to be serving as a body-guard for one of the trivia stars."

"Man, they are really taking this trivia tournament serious-ly," Carrie noted. "I can't figure out why."

"Trivia is popular."

"I know, but we've been warned at work that people are going to be flooding the beach bar, and we shouldn't plan on any of our shifts ending early."

Hali hadn't considered that. "I should probably put an extra person on each shift for the next week. We're going to be overrun if I don't."

"It can't hurt," Carrie agreed. "If you don't have enough bodies to cover everything, force your good-for-nothing brother to come in and help."

Hali frowned. Her brother Jesse wasn't exactly what she

would call a good worker. That didn't mean she wanted Carrie insulting him. "He's not so bad," she hedged.

"Please. If I was his mother, I would be cracking the whip. I'm not though."

"Let's talk about something else," Hali suggested. The day was going too well for her to focus on Jesse.

"Sure," Carrie replied, not missing a beat. "What's going on down the beach? Do you know who died?"

Whatever Hali was expecting, that wasn't it. She straightened, and immediately craned her neck to look down the beach in the direction she knew Carrie would've come from. Unfortunately for her, the palm trees were in her way. "What do you mean?"

"There's a whole crew of police officers down in front of the revolving restaurant," Carrie replied. "I thought you knew."

"No." Hali abandoned the rag on the table and edged out onto the sand. Still unable to see, she climbed onto one of the tables spread out across the beach and looked in the direction of the revolving restaurant. To her utter shock, her friend was right. There had to be at least four vehicles out on the beach ... and all of them had flashing lights. "Well, huh."

"I really did think you were aware," Carrie offered apologetically.

"Can you close that door for me?" Hali waved at the open tiki hut door. "I'm going to take a quick walk down the beach, just to check things out. You said there was a body?"

"The medical examiner is down there, so that's my assumption. I'll close the door," Carrie called out. "I will be back later to mercilessly tease you about how girly-girly you're turning out to be now that you have a boyfriend."

"I'm looking forward to it." Hali was completely focused on the flashing lights as she made her way down to the vehicles. The day was already hot—it was going to turn into a scorcher, which was normal for St. Pete Beach this time of year —but Hali barely noticed as she wiped the sweat off her forehead and surveyed the activity.

She couldn't see a body. At least not from her vantage point. Numerous people had stopped walking down the beach so they could watch the police officers work, but she didn't pay much attention to them either. She was more interested in the man standing in the center of all the mayhem. She recognized him.

Detective Andrew Copeland was friends with Gray. They had a solid relationship. Hali had met him long before she'd become involved with the taciturn private investigator, but she'd grown to know the man relatively well over the course of the past few months. Now, as he stood talking to someone from the medical examiner's office, Hali recognized that he was legitimately upset ... which meant something very bad had happened.

Perhaps sensing her watching him, Andrew shifted so he was looking at her. He held up a finger, telling her to stay put, and she patiently waited for another five minutes. When he tore away from the individual he'd been conversing with, he looked tired as he made his way to her.

"Is Gray with you?" he asked by way of greeting. He almost looked hopeful.

"No, but he's on the resort grounds," Hali replied. "He picked up a job for Franklin running security for an individual for an event. If you need him, though, I can get him down here."

Andrew hesitated and then shook his head. "That's okay. I'm sure he'll find me." He made an attempt at a smile and failed. "I'm sure you have questions."

"I'm just curious," Hali replied. "That's not one of my people, is it?"

"We don't have an identification yet, but I'm going to say

no." Andrew held up his phone so Hali could see a photo of the deceased. "You don't recognize him, do you?"

The man was young, not even thirty yet if Hali had to guess, and his brown eyes were wide and sightless. Hali could just make out his chest and the bloody mess there, so she knew they weren't dealing with some sort of accident. She could also make out the color of his shirt, and there was something about it that struck her as odd.

"Is he wearing a Daze Beer Trivia Challenge shirt?" she asked.

Andrew bobbed his head. "Yeah. Is that important?"

"I'm not sure." Hali glanced around. She could feel a suddenly chilly breeze on the back of her neck, and it was out of place given the heat and time of day. Nothing immediately stood out though. "We're the ones hosting that trivia competition this week. I don't know who that is, but if he was wearing the shirt..." She trailed off.

"Then the organizers of the trivia challenge should be able to help me identify him," Andrew surmised.

"Pretty much," Hali confirmed. "I mean, I can't guarantee it, but I think it's your best bet."

"No, it's a good tip. I didn't even think about the shirt." Andrew dragged a hand through his hair. "I appreciate it. You should be careful until we figure out what's going on too. I don't think Gray wants to lose you so soon after he found you."

"I know how to take care of myself," Hali assured him. "Can you tell me anything about the manner of death?"

Andrew hesitated, but only for a split second. "He was stabbed, Hali. It was bad. I don't know what time it happened. I don't have a motive because I don't have an ID yet. He has no wallet on him, so it could be a robbery."

The way he said it made Hali think he didn't mean it. "You believe otherwise though," she deduced.

He nodded. "This doesn't feel like a robbery. Keep your eyes open. I'll be in touch with Gray if I think there's something to worry about. Just ... watch your back."

"Oh, if I didn't know better, I would think that you have a crush on me," Hali teased.

"I think you're great." Andrew was guileless when responding. "Absolutely amazing. It's the way you've made my friend's life better that's important to me though. The way Gray looks at you ... well ... I've never seen him this happy."

Hali's cheeks caught fire. "He makes me happy too."

"Good. That means you'll watch his back and your own to keep him happy."

"I most definitely will." When Hali turned to head back to the tiki bar, she was smacked in the face with another cool breeze. It was under the palm trees near the bar that she finally found a source. There, one of the dark merrow that had been stalking her for weeks at this point stood and watched the scene play out.

Hali didn't know his name. She didn't even know if the dark merrow had names. She recognized the face though. It was the merrow who had stopped to visit her at the tiki bar not long after she'd fought off a mirror monster. He'd warned of bad things to come, and now here he was, watching the police work a murder scene.

She didn't cross to him. She knew better. Instead, she watched with a feeling of dread as he lifted his hand and waved at her. It was a taunt. Plain and simple. He was taunting her.

Why, though? Hali couldn't say. Instead, she remained rooted to her spot and waited for the dark merrow to disappear. She was brave and always ready for a fight. This was an enemy she couldn't yet read, however.

It was better to be safe than sorry. Especially now that she had Gray. Together, they were a fearsome force. She would not ruin his life by running headlong into danger on her own. She wasn't stupid, and she wasn't about to change when it came to something so fundamental.

She would have to wait to confront the merrow. She needed a time when she wasn't the vulnerable one. She didn't care how long she had to wait. The opportunity would come about eventually. She was almost certain of it.

FOUR

Gray had no doubt the rules he'd saddled Dominic with were going to be ignored. One meeting with the guy was all he needed to know that things between the two of them were going to be rough. He was so convinced things were going to get ugly that he considered dropping the job altogether.

Then he walked out to the sidewalk that led to Hali's bar and saw the commotion on the beach. His heart instantly plunged to his stomach, and he found himself heading in that direction.

Gray was an investigator. He knew crime scenes well. The first thing he saw when he moved beyond the palm trees was a coroner's van. The second thing he saw—or, well, scented was more precise—was Hali.

She stood in the shade of a palm tree watching the emergency responders work. There was a body bag being loaded into a van, something that gave Gray pause, but his momentum took him toward her.

"Hali."

She jerked up her head when she heard him and smiled.

The expression might have seemed out of place, but he knew it was only for him. He automatically extended an arm and drew her close when he neared, pressing a kiss to the top of her head before pulling back far enough to study her face.

"What happened?" he asked.

"I'm not entirely certain." Hali was grim as she regarded him. "Andrew is working over there, but he didn't have a lot of time for me."

"I have time for you." Gray rubbed his hand up and down her back as he regarded his friend. He could tell by the muscle working in Andrew's jaw that the detective was tense. Gray was determined to figure out exactly what was going on regardless, however. "We'll just wait here for a few minutes. If he doesn't come over to us, I'll go over to him."

Hali nodded, her fingers lightly wrapping around Gray's wrist. It was an unconscious reaction that Gray found interesting, although he didn't comment on it.

"How was your meeting with Dominic Lawson?" Hali asked after several minutes of silence.

"He's a complete and total tool," Gray replied, not missing a beat. "Like ... a complete and total tool. If you look up the word 'douche' in the dictionary, it's his picture you find."

"I take it you're no longer working for Franklin," Hali said on a laugh.

Gray only regarded her for a split second before he responded. "No. I didn't quit."

"You didn't?" Hali's eyes widened as she looked her boyfriend up and down. "I thought for sure you were going to quit right away."

Gray could see that. He had no intention of quitting though. "The money is too good to quit."

Hali made a face. "That's not why you're taking the job. I mean ... you might be happy with the money. You're taking it because of me though, and you know it."

"I didn't realize you'd developed an interest in security," Gray replied, not missing a beat. "I guess you learn something new every day."

Hali made a face. "Don't." She wagged her finger. "When we got involved, the only rule was that we tell each other the truth. I don't expect you to be beholden to me. You don't even have to fill me in on your new job. Just don't lie to me."

Gray frowned. He hated that she had a point. "Fine. I want to stick close to you. Sue me."

Hali's expression slid into a smirk. "I think it's kind of cute."

"You would." Gray rested his forehead against hers. "I like the idea of being here all week. I'll have a job to do." He linked his fingers with hers. "You'll have a job to do. At night, we'll be able to spend time together. I won't have to run to and from the resort. I'll just be here. With you."

"Oh, that's very sweet," a male voice said from behind Gray's back, causing the shifter to jolt.

When Gray turned, he found Andrew watching them with amused eyes. "If you're going to start messing with me, you should know that I don't care about being teased." He kept a firm grip on Hali's hand. "I'm happy, and nothing is going to change that."

"I'm glad that you're happy." Andrew said it in perfunctory fashion, but there was a glint to his eyes. "Actually, I'm *really* glad that you're happy."

Gray had no doubt that his friend meant it. "What's up with the dead guy?"

"They don't have an ID yet," Hali volunteered, catching Gray off guard.

"We do now," Andrew replied, turning grim. "Thanks to Hali's tip about the trivia tournament being held here, we went through the Daze Beer employee rosters. They have photos on their website."

"You gave them a tip?" Gray queried of Hali.

"He's wearing a trivia shirt," Hali replied. "I told him about the tournament. That's all I had though."

"And you found someone on the website that matches your victim?" Gray asked Andrew.

"Yup." Andrew bobbed his head and held up his phone. "Brian Parker."

Gray leaned in so he could study the face in the photo. "Wait ... I think I saw this guy last night."

"At my bar?" Hali asked, her forehead creasing as she studied the photo. "I don't recognize him."

"It wasn't at the bar. It was when we were walking home. We were in the parking lot, and you mentioned how pretty the moon was. Then we ... um ... talked with our faces a little closer. I saw that guy cutting through the trees on his way away from the hotel when we pulled apart."

"You talked with your faces a little closer?" Andrew demanded. "That is the most ridiculous thing I've ever heard."

Gray glared at him. "Don't give me grief."

"You're so whipped." Andrew managed a smile despite the dour circumstances. Then he sobered. "Do you think this guy was following you?"

Gray searched his memory and then shook his head. "No, I really don't. He barely looked at us. It was more that he was startled we were out there."

"Making out like teenagers," Andrew added helpfully.

Gray pretended he hadn't heard his friend as Hali giggled. "He wasn't interested in us. He was going somewhere, although I obviously have no idea where."

"Well, it's still a place to look." Andrew flicked his gaze to Hali. "I don't suppose you have a timetable for the arrivals of these trivia people, do you?"

"Oh, um, let me think." Hali tapped her bottom lip with a finger on the hand Gray wasn't holding. "I know that some of the workers for the group started arriving yesterday," she said after several seconds. "I don't know about the contestants though," she admitted. "I haven't cared enough to dig too much. I figured they wouldn't be a problem."

Gray watched as the body bag was loaded into the coroner's van. "It appears they are going to be trouble after all."

"We have no reason to believe that this is tied to the trivia contest right now," Andrew cautioned. "All I know is that our victim was stabbed and that he's on the trivia website as an employee. While it's possible that this had something to do with the contest, it's also possible that it had nothing to do with it."

Hali nodded. "Will you let us know when you find out?"

"I will." Andrew sent her a soft smile.

"Then I'll head back up to the bar. I'm late getting it open." She sent a searching look toward Gray. "Will you stop by before you head back to your new charge?"

"I most definitely will." Gray leaned in and gave her a quick kiss. If Andrew hadn't been present, it would've lingered. He had the grace to keep his friend from seeing too much tongue though. "I'll just be a few minutes behind you."

"Okay." Hali waved at Andrew before heading up the beach.

Gray and Andrew watched her go for several silent seconds. Then, as if sensing that Andrew's attention had shifted, Gray glanced at his friend.

"What?"

"I didn't say anything." Andrew held up his hands in mock surrender. "You look happy though."

On a different day, when he was feeling like a different man, Gray might've been annoyed by the statement. That's not how he felt today, however. "I feel pretty happy. Well, other than the dead body." He was calm as he focused on the police detective. "What can you tell me? There has to be something that you're leaving out."

"There really isn't," Andrew replied. "We don't have much to go on. We're going to track down the trivia people next. I'll let you know when I find anything out."

"I really appreciate it." Gray meant it. "I'm going to be sticking close to the resort for the next few days, so if you need anything from me, I'll be here."

"With your girlfriend."

"With my Hali," Gray confirmed. "Don't give me grief over it. Even if you do, though, nothing is going to change. I like her too much."

"I'm not going to give you grief." Andrew was calm. "I like that you're smiling again. It's been a long time. If she's the reason for that smile, then I kind of love her."

"She's fun."

"And you're gone over her," Andrew deduced. "I can see it."

Gray could've denied it. There was no point, though. "And I'm gone over her," he confirmed.

"Which means you're going to stick close until the killer is caught."

"Yup." Gray saw no sense denying it. "That means I want you to keep me in the loop."

"I'll do my best."

Gray hummed to himself as he trudged toward the tiki bar. Hali was a hummer, although there were times he was convinced she didn't realize that. Now that they were spending so much time together, he'd become a hummer too. He was about to bring it up, maybe even serenade Hali with a song before the bar started filling up, and then he realized that his girlfriend wasn't alone.

He scowled as he picked up his pace, plopping himself onto the stool to Dominic's right before the man even registered his presence. "I thought you were staying up in your room."

Inside the tiki hut, Hali dried a glass with a towel and watched the interaction with overt amusement. She did not, however, interject herself into the conversation.

"Well, *Dad*, I decided that some fresh air might be in order," Dominic drawled as he sipped the cocktail he'd ordered from Hali before Gray's arrival. "I didn't realize I wasn't allowed out on the grounds."

"We discussed this," Gray insisted. "You're supposed to provide me with a schedule so we can come up with a plan. We just talked about this."

"And I'm a grown man," Dominic pointed out. "Grown men get to do what they want to do." He shot a charming smile at Hali. "Isn't that right, doll?"

Hali didn't immediately respond, instead putting the glass away before grabbing a different one and filling it with iced tea for Gray. She was silent as she slid the tea toward him.

"I didn't say you weren't a grown man," Gray replied. "I just want you to be careful. There's a dead body on the beach."

"Really?" Dominic perked up. "Anybody I know?"

"I don't know. Does the name Brian Parker ring any bells?"

Dominic tilted his head, considering, and then shook it. "Sorry, but no."

Gray was only mildly disappointed. "He worked for the trivia company. We're not quite sure why he was targeted yet. We should know more in a few hours. Until then, you shouldn't wander around on your own."

"Unless I'm mistaken, Mr. Craven hired you to watch me because I tend to tick off boyfriends and husbands," Dominic pointed out. "Murder wasn't on the menu."

"Just ... tell me when you go somewhere," Gray shot back, his annoyance on full display.

"Fine. I'm going to go to the promised land right now," Dominic said, his eyes swinging to Hali. "Would you like to go to the promised land with me?"

"Oh, what a sweet offer," Hali replied before Gray could wrap his hands around Dominic's throat and start squeezing. "I'm good though."

Dominic made a "come on" sound deep in his throat. "How can you say that? Look at me. I'm young, single, and ready to mingle. Don't you want to mingle with me?" There was a coyness to the way he batted his eyelashes that set Gray's teeth on edge.

"Don't use your magic on her," Gray warned.

Dominic's mouth dropped open. "Um ... you can't use the M-word in front of people I don't know." He looked horrified. "How would you like it if I spread your secret around the resort? Granted, I don't exactly know what the secret is right now, but I'll totally find out and spread it. You wouldn't like it very much if I shared it with this beautiful young lady, would you?"

Gray's annoyance had teeth. "First off, Hali is aware of the magical world." He didn't add that Hali was also magical. He didn't feel it was necessary. "Secondly, I don't really have any secrets. Especially from her." He pointed at his girlfriend.

For a supposed trivia god, Dominic wasn't very quick on the uptake, Gray decided. The man looked genuinely baffled. "I'm not sure I understand," he hedged.

"Then let me spell it out for you." Gray was matter of fact. "Hali is my girlfriend. Now, she's her own person and makes her own decisions, but if you hit on her, I'm going to be mad." He leaned close so Dominic would have no other option but to stare into his eyes. "You won't like me when I get mad."

"Okay, Incredible Hulk," Dominic drawled on a laugh,

shaking his head. "I didn't realize you were together." He shifted his attention to Hali. "I wonder if that's why my powers didn't work on you." He said it more to himself than her, but he seemed genuinely curious.

"I thought it was against the rules to use your magic on others," Gray demanded.

"I'm not trying to force her to do anything she doesn't want to do," Dominic shot back. "I just have a natural ability to draw people in. It's like I exert a musk."

"I think I might gag," Gray complained as Hali grinned.

"People are drawn to me because of said musk," Dominic explained. "I can't explain it. The good news for you is that your girl didn't even react to it."

"And why would that be?" Hali asked. She looked genuinely interested.

"I'm not sure." Dominic tapped his fingers on the bar as he considered the question. "You're clearly magical. Are you a witch?"

Hali nodded. "I am."

"I figured." Dominic smiled. "Some witches are immune to my magic. Not all of them, though. Are you a powerful witch?"

Hali lifted one shoulder in a shrug. "I'm not sure. I guess that depends on your definition of powerful."

Dominic switched his attention to Gray and waited.

"She's powerful," Gray confirmed. "I've never been around a more powerful witch."

"Is that saying much?" Dominic asked.

"I've been around my fair share of witches," he replied. "She's the best."

Hali's cheeks colored under the praise, and she immediately went back to cleaning her glassware.

"Aw, so cute," Dominic trilled, shaking his head and rolling his eyes. "If she's powerful enough, she can hold off my musk. I don't think that's the reason she didn't respond in this case though."

"Oh, yeah?" Gray was interested despite his determination to hate the guy. "And why is that?"

"It's you."

Gray's eyebrows hiked toward his hairline. "Me?"

"Yes, you," Dominic agreed. "You're gumming up her works. She's so full of you, she can't see anybody else."

"What does that mean?" Hali asked as she rested her elbows on the bar. "Are you saying my attachment to Gray means other magics can't touch me?"

"My magic is mind magic," Dominic reminded her. "If your mind—and heart in this case—are completely consumed by others, there's no infiltrating either. You basically have a 'no vacancy' sign up on your hotel. He's the only guest allowed."

Hali choked on a laugh. "That is an interesting way to describe it. Do you think I have a 'no vacancy' sign up?"

"I don't care as long as I'm the one in the penthouse suite." Gray winked at her. "Either way, it's interesting to know."

"I find it distressing," Dominic countered. "I mean ... she's the hottest woman here, I bet. She's the resort princess if you will. Knowing she's already taken is a total bummer."

"Well, she's already taken." Gray was having none of it as he regarded the downtrodden trivia guru. "If you want to hit on someone, it's not going to be her. In fact, you'd better make sure it's not somebody who is already taken. I don't want to spend the entire week saving you from getting your ass kicked."

"I am intrigued," Hali admitted, shifting so she was closer to Dominic. "If I have a 'no vacancy' sign up, how is it that you've managed to get into so much trouble with others who should also have 'no vacancy' signs up?"

"Because not all people commit the same way," Dominic

replied. "You two are clearly in the early stages of your relationship. You're infatuated with one another. I've seen it a million times."

"So, you're saying I won't always have a 'no vacancy' sign up," Hali surmised, her disappointment obvious.

"I am not saying that." Dominic vehemently shook his head. "There's always a shine on people who are in a new relationship. Some people retain that shine, and others don't. Those who don't are my bread and butter. Those who do remain strong forever. I'm willing to bet you guys are examples of the latter. You'll have to wait it out though."

"Like soul mates?" Gray queried.

Dominic looked as if he was rapidly losing interest in the conversation. "Maybe, but I haven't given it that much thought. You guys are clearly only interested in each other right now. That might change. It might not."

Gray knew deep down that it wouldn't change. He kept that to himself, though. For now. "Well, it's an interesting tidbit to consider. Perhaps you could only point your magic at the 'no vacancy' signs this week, huh?" he asked Dominic.

"Yeah, I wouldn't bet on that being the case," Dominic replied.

"I had to try."

"You were doomed for failure, my friend. That's not how I roll."

That's exactly what Gray was afraid of.

FIVE

Dominic showed no signs of wanting to leave the tiki bar, which was fine with Gray because being close to Hali was the lone perk to this job as far as he could tell. Sure, the money was nice, but he wasn't hurting in that department. If it weren't for the prospect of being able to see Hali throughout the day, he would've declined the job. Now that a body had appeared on the beach, however, he was glad to have taken it.

"I talked Rusty into going to my place and picking up some clothes for me," Gray volunteered when Hali returned to the tiki hut with a tray of empty cups. "He's going to drop them in the patio area behind the villa if that's okay with you."

"That's fine," Hali replied automatically. "He can drop them off here if that's easier. We can put the bag under the counter until we head back tonight."

Gray hesitated and then nodded. "He might like that. He's been making noise about seeing you again."

"Does he know we're together?"

"He does. He's been teasing me mercilessly about it. He's still convinced that he's going to somehow talk Carrie into going on a date with him and wants to set up a meal for the four of us."

Hali snorted. "He doesn't have the right parts to entice Carrie."

"That won't stop him from trying."

"Well, he can go ahead and try. It might be funny to watch." Hali started tossing the cups she'd returned with into the garbage. Glass wasn't allowed on the patio. Only individuals sitting on the stools at the tiki hut drank out of regular glasses. That made cleanup easier. "Where's your new best friend?"

Gray scowled. "Don't call him that. He's a job. Nothing more."

"I find him interesting."

Gray's hackles went up at the simple statement. "Excuse me?"

"Oh, not like that." Hali's laugh was light. "I just found what he was saying about his powers not working on certain individuals interesting. I like the idea that I'm just so into you I couldn't possibly look at anybody else, even if magic is involved."

Gray hated to admit it, but he liked that idea too. "Yes, well, he's a turd. I don't want his turdiness rubbing off on our happiness."

Hali patted his forearm. "I think we'll be okay."

Gray nipped in for a kiss because he couldn't help himself, but the touching of lips was brief. When he sat again, the stool beside him had been filled by Lana Silver.

"Fun fact," she announced in her usual greeting. "On average, people spend about 336 hours of their lives kissing."

"Oh, yeah?" Gray arched an eyebrow as he reached for his iced tea. He liked Lana—she was too innocuous not to like— but she often made him uncomfortable. Her mind was extremely analytical, but he didn't always get her jokes. Heck, he didn't know if she realized she was making a joke at times. "I think we can do better than that." He winked at Hali.

"There are also arcane laws still on the books regarding kissing," Lana continued, not missing a beat. "For example, in Indiana, it is illegal for men with mustaches to habitually kiss human beings."

"Wow." Gray honestly had no idea how to respond.

"In Logan County—that's in Colorado—a man is forbidden to kiss a woman when she's asleep. And in some states, it's forbidden to kiss your wife on Sundays."

"Well, I'll need a list," Gray replied easily. "I'm going to kiss my woman whenever I feel like it. That means I'll have to be careful if I'm in the wrong state."

"Did you just call me your woman?" Hali demanded.

"Of course not." Gray didn't miss a beat. "I'm just saying should I ever have a woman all to myself, I'm going to kiss her whenever I want. If you don't want to be that woman, I guess I'll have to adjust."

"Oh, whatever." Hali rolled her eyes, but a small smile played at the corners of her lips. "What's going on, Lana? Are you excited about the trivia contest?"

"More than a hundred people are going to be participating," Lana replied. "There are preliminary rounds and everything." She looked earnest. "I hope I don't go out in the preliminary rounds. That would be embarrassing."

"Something tells me you're going to go far," Hali countered.

"Some of the biggest names in trivia are here though." Lana gnawed on her bottom lip. "They all know each other. They're all used to this. I've only played bar trivia and stuff. What if I falter under pressure?"

Gray watched Hali draw Lana's attention to her and smiled at the way his girlfriend soothed the other woman's obviously frazzled nerves.

"I suspect that you'll be nervous at first," Hali conceded. "I bet those nerves won't last all that long though. You just need to get past the first questions, and then you'll be fine."

"How can you know that?"

"I just do." Hali tilted her head to the side and indicated a table at the far corner of the patio area. "Those are trivia people, right? I saw you checking your phone when you were walking up."

"They are." Lana turned solemn. "Most of them have been on the televised trivia tournaments."

"So, give me a rundown," Hali instructed. "I want to know who I'm going to be waiting on."

Gray internally applauded Hali's machinations. He wanted to know as much as possible about the people who would be flooding the resort. Lana wasn't prone to gossip or histrionics. Everything she had on them would be factual. That was a good thing.

"That's David Kyle Hamburg," Lana started, pointing toward a tall blond man in a plaid shirt. It wasn't flannel, but it looked heavy for normal beach wear. "People call him DK."

"That's a weird shirt," Hali noted. "It's all pinks, yellows, and whites. His shorts are khaki too. With his hair and skin tone, he kind of looks like a human thumb."

"He's very smart." Lana solemnly bobbed her head. "People say his IQ is 170."

Hali didn't put a lot of stock in IQ tests. "Is that good?"

"It's pretty good."

Dominic picked that moment to return to the bar and order another drink. He'd obviously heard what they were talking about because he immediately inserted himself into the conversation.

"That dude is also a womanizer," he announced. "He picks one opponent to romance each cycle. He makes her think he's going to leave his wife for her, throws her off her game, and then proceeds to forget her name by the end of the tournament."

"He looks like a giant thumb," Hali complained, giving the man another once-over. "Why is anybody falling for him?"

Dominic held out his hands and shrugged. "I have no idea. People say he's superficially charming, but I've never seen it."

Even though Gray wanted to spend as little time as possible with Dominic, he realized the man's prominence in the trivia community—and his powers—would make him a solid source of gossip. "What about the others?" he asked, gesturing toward the table.

Dominic was more than happy to hop on a stool and spread his wealth of information. "I'm so glad you asked."

Hali and Gray exchanged amused looks, and Hali automatically reached for Dominic's cup so she could dump it and make him another cocktail.

"That's Cadence Carpenter." He pointed toward a petite brunette who was so pale she was almost transparent. "She's married to Niles Carpenter." He pointed toward a bland-looking man sitting next to her, arms crossed in defensive fashion. "Now, they talk endless crap about each other but present a united front when competing. They both have slots at this tournament."

"Do they cheat?" Gray asked.

"Not that I'm aware of. It's hard to cheat at trivia. Nobody can have their phones on their person during the event, and they have bouncers watching the crowd to make sure nobody is mouthing answers or anything. I'm sure they study together, but that can't really be considered cheating."

"No," Gray agreed. "What's their story?"

"Well, Niles is what you would call a milquetoast," Dominic replied. "He's essentially the vanilla yogurt of the trivia tour. He's boring. He does very little work. He goes to bed at ten o'clock every night. I heard he only owns white underwear, but I have no idea if that's true."

"Wouldn't he have to be showing his underwear to someone for that rumor to start?" Hali queried.

Dominic shrugged.

"I only ask because if he's a milquetoast, then he wouldn't be showing his underwear to anyone," Hali pressed.

"Good point." Dominic grinned. "I hadn't gotten that far. The guy is boring. There's no way around it. As for his wife, well, she's a different story. Depending on who you talk to, everybody has a different take on her."

"Well, we're dying to hear," Hali prodded.

"Some people say she's an introvert who is socially awkward and afraid of people," Dominic started. "Other people, however, say she's a rampant narcissist who could maybe even be a sociopath."

Oh, well, now he had Gray's attention. "Those are interesting takes on the same individual."

"They are," Dominic agreed. "The thing is, she's manipulative. Even if you believe she's awkward, there's no getting around how manipulative she is. She'll cry if somebody doesn't pay enough attention to her, but you never get the feeling that she's crying because her feelings are actually hurt."

"She's crying because she can't control the situation," Hali surmised.

Dominic nodded. "Exactamundo, my pretty little bartender." He winked.

"I'll thump you," Gray warned. "What did I say about flirting with her?"

"Oh, get over yourself." Dominic wasn't frightened in the least. "It's obvious she only has eyes for you. I can't stop myself from flirting, though. That's my default. You need to get over it."

"Whatever." Gray made a grumbling sound deep in his

throat. "What should we expect from them during the competition?"

"Not much." Dominic held out his hands. "They're usually peripheral to the drama. That's not to say they don't participate. They're just smart about it and never in the middle of things. They won't cause overt trouble. They might manipulate others to cause trouble, but if they do, you'll never be able to catch them in the act."

"Okay." Gray bobbed his head. "What about the tall blonde with the nice ... dress?"

Hali's mouth dropped open. "You weren't going to say dress," she accused.

Gray chuckled. "Of course I was. What else was I going to say?"

"You were going to say boobs," Hali shot back, refusing to back down.

"I would never say the B-word. It's not polite."

"Whatever." Hali was having none of it. "You don't have to pretend you don't see them. Those things are so ridiculous, they need their own zip code."

"That's Michelle Morris," Dominic volunteered. "She's thirty-six and still lives with her parents."

Gray straightened his neck. "She's thirty-six? She looks twenty-five."

"And she prides herself on that," Dominic confirmed. "She believes she can seduce any man. I purposely refuse to engage with her because it throws her off to the point where she misses questions. Nobody ever tells her no. She's started telling other people I'm gay because she can't wrap her head around the fact that someone might not be attracted to her."

"How come she still lives with her parents?" Hali queried. "That's weird at her age."

"Apparently, her parents live in a huge mansion, and she doesn't want to downgrade," Dominic replied. "She gets upset when anybody mentions that it's weird to still live with your parents voluntarily at that age."

"I think Gray likes what he sees," Hali said darkly, drawing Gray's attention back to her.

"Don't even," Gray warned. "I'm just trying to get a feel for the people we're dealing with. I only have eyes for you."

"He does," Dominic agreed, not missing a beat. "I've been watching him. The rest of this beach could be swallowed up by sand lizards, and he wouldn't take his eyes off you. It's a bit pathetic if you ask me."

"Nobody asked you," Gray growled.

"What about her?" Hali asked, pointing toward a strawberry blonde at the far end of the table. "I've been watching them, and I could've basically guessed just about every other detail you provided on the others. I might not have figured out that the blonde was still living with her parents, but the rest of it is pretty obvious. She's different though."

"She *is* different," Dominic confirmed. "That's Vinessa Dawson. She goes by Vinnie and holds herself out as 'one of the guys'." He offered up the appropriate air quotes. "She's an empty void."

Hali cocked her head. "Meaning what?"

"Meaning that she only puts surface things on display. There's nothing deep about her."

"Are you saying she doesn't have a soul?" Gray asked.

"I don't know the specifics of creatures with or without souls," Dominic replied. "That's not my thing. I just know she too is immune to my powers."

"That could just mean she has good taste," Hali said dryly, eliciting a grin from Gray.

"It's not that." Dominic looked legitimately troubled as he shook his head. "They say she's married, and I have seen her with a wedding ring a time or two, but she doesn't act married.

The guy you think looks like a thumb? She's kind of like him, but somehow lesser. It's hard to explain."

"Try," Gray prodded.

"She flirts with any man who will show her attention. I'm fine with that because I like a flirty woman. Sometimes she flirts with women too."

"Maybe she's bisexual," Hali suggested.

"Maybe, and it would be hot if I could get behind that assumption. That's not the feeling I get from her though. She likes to win. She manipulates both men and women. She has relationships on the surface. Unfortunately for her, none of those relationships seem to have deep roots as far as I can tell."

Dominic stared hard for several seconds and then shook himself out of his reverie. "I just know she gives me the creeps. We're pleasant in public, but we're not friends. If you asked any of those people over there, they would tell you they're not friends with her either. She's just not always there even when she's there."

"She's an empty shell," Hali said, understanding finally washing over her features. "Maybe that makes her one to watch."

Gray had been thinking the same thing. "Is there anybody in that group you consider a legitimate threat to your victory?"

"Not so much," Dominic replied. "They say Cathy Thompson will be here before the end of the day. I could see her taking the crown if she's motivated, but she's not always motivated."

"And what's her story?" Gray asked.

"She's a dominant beast who likes to get into her enemies' heads and do real damage before the tournament." Dominic sipped his drink and then offered up a wide smile. "Basically, she's the female version of me."

That was a terrifying thought, Gray mused as Dominic headed off to rejoin the others at the table. He seemed to have no problem talking smack and then hanging out with them as if he didn't have a care in the world.

"What do you think?" Hali asked as she appeared at his side.

Gray's arm automatically went around her waist. "I'm not sure. We have no proof any of these people are responsible for what happened to the guy on the beach. That could have nothing to do with the tournament. It could be a random act of violence."

"It could," Hali agreed. "The thing is random acts of violence are very rarely random. I would believe that guy was targeted by someone he knew rather than happening upon a murderous stranger any day of the week. I think there's more to be discovered about these people."

"You read my mind." Gray pressed a kiss to her temple. "I'm going to move over to that table in the shade so I can eavesdrop on them while running their names through my search database at the same time. It can't possibly hurt if I'm already here working."

"That sounds like a plan. Let me know if you need me to charge your phone. I'll be trying to elicit information from them throughout the day too."

"Okay." Gray pursed his lips so he could draw her in for a kiss. "I like working together. It's kind of fun."

"You're going to be bored in two hours flat," Hali countered. "You're stuck now though."

"Well, at least I have something pretty to look at while I'm stuck."

Hali laughed as she swatted away his wandering hands. "Be good," she admonished. "We still have five hours until we close down for the night. It's going to be a long day."

"It will be fine." Gray meant it. "When you're ready to close things down, I'll escort Dominic back to his room and then come back for you. I just texted Rusty and he says he'll be bringing my clothes by right as you're shutting down. If we're not here, he'll come over to the villa."

"It will be okay regardless," Hali promised. "I think, once you return your charge to his room and I close up here, that maybe pizza is in order. We can spend some time on my back patio cuddling too. If you're so inclined, I mean."

"Cuddling?" Laughter bubbled up and grabbed him by the throat. "I think that can be arranged."

"Good." She leaned close for two seconds and then pulled back. "It's nice having you here." She said it in her softest voice, and it touched his very soul.

"My perfect day is spent with you right now, so it is nice." He tucked a strand of flyaway hair behind her ear. "I'll be here if you need anything. Don't work that hip too hard. That's my job for when it's time to cuddle."

"I'll try to refrain."

"You do that."

Six

"You stay here," Gray ordered Hali when it was time to walk Dominic back to his room upon the closing of the Salty Cauldron. She was favoring her hip, although she would never admit that out loud. "I'm being serious."

The look Hali shot him was straight out of a horror movie. "I'll do what I want when I want."

"Hali." Gray sounded pained. "Just ... wait for me, huh?"

"So you can carry me?"

That was indeed what Gray had in mind, although he didn't want to say it in mixed company because he knew she would react poorly to the admission. "Maybe I want to hold your hand and get frisky in the sand before we go. Have you ever considered that?"

Hali snorted. "Please. You prefer getting frisky in places where sand can't creep into your nether regions. Give me a break."

"Hey! I'm adventurous."

"Yeah, yeah, yeah." Hali waved him off. "If you hurry, I'll

still be here when you get back. If not, you'll know where to find me."

Irritation bubbled up, but Gray knew better than to give it voice. "Fine, if you want to fight before the pizza, I'm up for it. I'm still going to *From Here to Eternity* you at some point. You've been warned."

"I'm looking forward to it." Hali went back to cleaning the tables outside the bar.

Gray cast one more worried look over his shoulder before falling into step with Dominic. Despite the seemingly endless stream of cocktails he'd imbibed, Dominic only appeared mildly buzzed.

"Why are you so worried about her?" Dominic asked as they headed down the sidewalk. "She seems pretty capable. And, well, it's the beach. How much trouble can she find at the beach?"

"You would be surprised." Gray looked back at her one more time and then sighed. "She can take care of herself with other people. That's not what I'm worried about."

"So, it's her hip," Dominic surmised. "I wondered."

Gray slowed his pace. "How do you know about that?"

"I'm an air elemental with mind magic. Pain is an emotion that's hard to hide, no matter how good or practiced you are at covering. I caught a few momentary twinges from her when she was passing by delivering drinks."

"Oh." Gray didn't know what to say, so he said nothing.

"How was she hurt?" Dominic asked.

"She was hit by a golf cart." Gray knew better than sharing the specifics, especially with a blabbermouth like Dominic. Franklin would melt down, and he didn't want to cause problems for Hali. "She needs surgery. She's reticent. I'm working on it."

"Have you considered bringing in a shaman?"

Gray wasn't expecting the question. Actually, he wasn't

expecting Dominic to think about anybody but himself because it went against his nature. The fact that he was so interested in Hali's health was both heartwarming and suspicious. Ultimately, the notion of helping Hali outweighed his mistrust of the trivia guru. "How could a shaman help?"

"They're mystical healers," Dominic replied. "I'm not guaranteeing they could do anything, but I'm betting if you get the right one that it would at least alleviate the pain she's constantly feeling, even if the defect isn't fully healed."

It was something Gray had never considered, and he was intrigued. "Tell me more."

Dominic chuckled. "You've got it bad, don't you? Don't bother denying it. I can see it written all over your face whenever you're around her."

"I do have it bad." Gray would never deny it. "She's ... amazing."

"She's pretty cool," Dominic agreed. "She's smoking hot and smart. She's also funny. It's rare to get the whole package. You should hold on to her."

"That's the plan."

"Although, you're a shifter," Dominic mused. "Will your pack even allow you to marry a witch?"

"I'm not pack. Even if I were, there's nothing that could keep me away from her."

"I like a freethinker. Maybe this arrangement won't be so bad. We can be friends and everything."

"I wouldn't go that far."

"It was worth a try."

HALI HAD TO REST HER HIP THREE TIMES to finish her cleanup. She hated how fatigued she felt by the end of her shift most nights, but she wasn't ready to embrace the idea of surgery ... even if she had been reading up on it on the sly. She didn't want to tell Gray about her new reading habits and get his hopes up. She wasn't quite there yet.

After one more thorough search of the patio area, she locked the tiki hut and moved to sit at one of the tables. Despite her bold words to Gray, she had no intention of torturing him and returning to the villa on her own. She would wait. Getting her jollies by freaking him out wasn't an acceptable option in her book.

"Is this seat taken?" an oily voice asked from her left, jolting her out of her reverie. When Hali looked up, she found the dark merrow she'd seen on the beach watching her.

"The bar is closed," she said evenly as she regarded him.

"I don't need a drink." He sat in the chair across from her without invitation. "You look like you had a busy evening. I must confess, it's after my bedtime. I wanted to approach you sooner, but there was never a good time."

"It's probably best you didn't," Hali agreed. She kept her hands on her lap in case she needed to use her magic and forced herself to breathe evenly. "On the surface, you pass for human. If somebody spends too much time in your presence, however, it becomes apparent that you're something else."

"I've been alive for a very long time," the merrow replied. "Sometimes humanity begins to look like something else when your mask gets old."

"Ah, well, what a lovely thought." Hali leaned back in her chair. Gray wouldn't return for at least ten minutes. If she wanted answers from the merrow, now was the time to get them. "Do you live here? In St. Pete, I mean."

"For now."

"For now?"

"That's what I said." His eyes narrowed. "What about you? Have you ever considered selecting a different beach to call home?"

"Not really. I've spent time in Tampa, but I really do

prefer St. Pete. It's just a personal thing. I love the way the water rolls out here. I can't explain it."

"I too happen to love the Gulf over the bay. When I try to swim in the bay, it's like being trapped in a cage. When I swim in the Gulf, however, it feels like freedom."

"I guess I can see that." Hali moved her right hand to the top of the table and began to restlessly drum her fingers. "You obviously want something. I saw you down on the beach earlier. Are you responsible for what happened to Brian Parker?"

"You'll have to be more specific. I'm not sure who that is."

"The dead guy you were watching get loaded into the coroner's van."

"Ah, that was just a coincidence." The merrow waved one pasty hand in dismissive fashion. "I was merely taking my morning walk and happened to come across the scene."

Hali didn't believe him. The problem was, he was a powerful paranormal creature. He didn't need a knife to kill. She couldn't quite fathom why he would kill some random trivia contest worker on the beach. "Are you aware of any other dangerous individuals in town right now?"

"No, but I don't concern myself with the day-to-day living of other creatures. I'm too old to care."

"And yet here you are with me." Hali's tone was dark. "It seems you're saying one thing and doing another."

"Well, you're different, aren't you?" the merrow queried. "You, my dear, are powerful. You also surround yourself with powerful friends. That shifter who is always with you doesn't even realize just how powerful he is right now. He will though, before it's all said and done. I'm looking forward to that day."

Hali had questions. By asking too many of them, she would be giving the merrow power she didn't want to cede. Instead, she merely pursed her lip and nodded. "That sounds like fun. I hope I'm there when that happens too."

"Something tells me you will be." The merrow's expression darkened. "I guess it's time we get down to business."

"That is preferable to whatever you're doing now," Hali readily agreed.

"I think it's time to draw up terms," the merrow continued, ignoring her snark. "We could undoubtedly fight a war—your faction against my faction—and one side will come out victorious. Both sides will incur losses should it go down that way, however. I would like to avoid that."

"Oh, really?" Hali was caught between amusement and irritation. "And what did you have in mind?"

"You will cede St. Pete to us, and we will give Tampa to you." The offer was made in light fashion, as if they were about to exchange bagged lunches in the kindergarten cafeteria.

"And why would I want to do that?" Hali demanded. "I already told you that I prefer St. Pete."

"Yes, and you have a business here," the merrow agreed. "I know that leaving this place would be difficult. It would, however, allow you to keep your army intact. Isn't that what you want?"

"I'm pretty sure I want to keep my business too. My home is here."

Annoyance sparked in the merrow's eyes, but his voice was calm when he spoke again. "Perhaps you didn't hear me. I'm offering you a chance to save those you love. Why not take it?"

"No, you're offering to let me retreat after I've given you this place," Hali shot back. "That's not something I'm willing to do. I have no idea what your plans are for this area, but I'm not going to sit back and let you hurt innocent people."

"And why would I possibly want to do that?"

"I have no idea. You're the bad guy, though. You're the muahaha type. All you're missing is a mustache to twirl. Your motivations really don't matter to me. I'm not going to step back and let you take over this beach. It's simply not going to happen."

"Well, that's rather disappointing. I can't say I'm surprised though. Everything we've learned about you suggests you'll be a stubborn mule."

"I idle at stubborn," Hali agreed.

They eyed each other with rampant distaste, their fingers drumming the same beat on the table. The tension was thicker than the fog that was fighting to roll in. Just when Hali was certain the merrow was going to make a move on her, footsteps sounded on the walkway. She didn't look away from the merrow when speaking.

"We're closed," she said automatically.

"That's a bummer, but I'm guessing you can open for your future brother-in-law," a gregarious voice replied.

Hali slowly shifted her gaze to Rusty, who had a suitcase in his hand and a concerned look on his face. Unlike his brother, Rusty was pack. Unlike the rest of his pack, Rusty refused to cut ties with his brother. He was a fun-loving individual with a loyal streak a mile wide, and Hali had no doubt he was willing to put his life on the line for her—simply because it was what his brother would want—should it become necessary. The look he was gracing the dark merrow with told her that Rusty was going to find it necessary if she didn't de-escalate the moment.

"You picked up Gray's clothes?" she asked, hoping her tone was coming across as light.

"I did." Rusty's gaze was on the merrow. "I didn't grab any of his standard boxer shorts though. I stopped at a store and bought him some really loud boxer shorts that he'll hate but you'll love."

"That sounds like a brother," she said on a hollow laugh.

"Yeah." Rusty put the suitcase in front of the tiki bar and stepped closer. "Where is my brother?"

"He's walking his charge back to his room," Hali replied. "I expect him back at any moment."

"Okay." Rusty linked his fingers together and cracked his knuckles in dramatic fashion. The threat in the gesture was obvious. "Who is your friend?"

"I wouldn't call him a friend," Hali replied. "He's more of an acquaintance. He stopped by when I was closing up."

"Oh, yeah?" Rusty cocked his head and showed the merrow his teeth. "How about you come over here, Hali?" he suggested. "I think I want to have a talk with your friend."

Hali was used to the testosterone flexing associated with shifters. Gray was nowhere near as bad as his brother. She wasn't in the mood today though. "I think I've got it," she assured him. "You were just going, correct?" she said to the merrow.

The merrow hesitated, glancing between Hali and Rusty, and then got to his feet. "I am leaving. My offer stands, however, Ms. Waverly. This beach isn't big enough for the both of us. At some point, one of us is going to have to go."

Rusty made a snarling sound that surprised Hali. She'd never known him to be anything other than fun and friendly, even in the face of danger. Now, though, he looked as if he was considering ripping the merrow's head off with his bare hands. "Don't you threaten her," he warned in a dark voice.

"It would be best if you didn't issue directives you can't enforce," the merrow announced as he stood. "You are not your brother. He is ten times the threat you are, even if he doesn't realize it yet. The witch is stronger than you, too."

"Is that a fact?" Rusty snarled. "Would you care to place a wager on that?"

"You're not even worth my time," the merrow said, exasperation lacing every word as he tutted and shook his head. "Call off your dog, Ms. Waverly, or I'll euthanize him."

Hali leaped to her feet and threw herself in front of Rusty

before the shifter could react and get himself killed. She had a feeling that's exactly what the merrow wanted. Rusty's annoyed howl was still reverberating when another figure appeared from between two palm trees.

It was another merrow—Hali recognized that right away —but she hadn't been aware of the creature's presence. She hadn't seen this creature before—she was almost positive— but if he was around, that meant others could be too.

"What's going on?" Gray asked as he joined the party. He was on the sidewalk, the new merrow—he looked to be a younger merrow—standing between him and Hali. His eyes were keen as he scanned faces, and it wasn't hard for him to figure out exactly what had gone down. Rusty was in attack mode, and Hali was desperate to keep him from throwing himself at the older merrow.

"Rusty, don't," Gray ordered.

Rusty, who had been practically salivating at the prospect of ripping the merrow limb from limb, immediately ceased trying to get around Hali. Instead, he tugged her to his side so he could stand as a shield.

Annoyed, Hali shot him a dark look. "I don't need your protection."

"Shh." Rusty touched his finger to her lips. "Just sit there and look pretty, okay?"

Hali's mouth dropped open as she turned toward Gray, but her boyfriend was already shaking his head.

"He's just posturing, Hali," he barked. "Don't let him get to you." Gray gave the younger merrow a wide berth as he closed the distance between himself and the other members of the group. "What do you want?" he snapped.

"I've already given my demands to Ms. Waverly. I'm sure she can share them with you." The merrow cast another dismissive look toward Rusty before starting toward the beach. "I'll be in touch."

"I'm not giving you this beach," Hali warned.

"You will before it's all said and done."

Hali didn't speak again as the merrow disappeared into the night. The younger merrow wordlessly followed. She sucked in oxygen at regular intervals, clenched and unclenched her fists, and waited.

"What was that?" Gray growled when he was reasonably assured the merrow were gone, none left to eavesdrop.

"I'm not sure," Rusty replied. "I brought your suitcase like you asked—I'm not your assistant by the way, bro—and found Hali sitting at a table with that ... that ... thing. What was that thing by the way? I could feel the evil permeating off him, but I have never felt anything similar in my entire life."

"It's a merrow," Hali replied in a low voice.

"Like a mermaid?" Rusty's forehead creased. "He didn't look like any mermaid I've ever seen."

"That's because you're getting the merrow confused with sirens," Hali replied, feigning patience. "They're different. Very different in fact."

"Just think of them as evil sea creatures," Gray replied. "That's what I've been doing. We haven't seen them in weeks. Not since the immediate aftermath of the mirror monster fiasco. I was kind of hoping they weren't coming back."

"They're not going anywhere until we make them go somewhere," Hali replied. "He made that very clear just now."

Gray strode to her, his hand slipping over the back of her head so he could stare into her eyes. "He didn't hurt you, did he?"

"No, he did not," Hali assured him. "I'm perfectly fine. He just wanted to talk."

"About what?" Rusty queried. "Did he really think you were just going to give him the beach?"

"He did seem to think that," Hali confirmed. "He was irritated when I didn't even entertain the possibility. He says there's going to be a war, and it's better to agree to a truce before we start firing missiles at one another."

"And what did you say to that?" Gray asked.

"What do you think I said?"

He smirked. "I think you told him to stuff it." Gray pressed a kiss to her forehead and then pulled her in for a hug. "I don't like that he waited until I was gone to approach you. That feels pointed."

"He admitted to watching me all night," Hali said. "He didn't want to approach when there were guests at the bar."

"Then we—and by we, I mean you—need to come up with better wards for this bar. I don't like that he can approach you whenever he wants."

"I'll give it some thought. Over pizza."

Gray smirked. "Fine, but we're eating the pizza in bed." He gave her a soft kiss.

"Oh, well this is just gross," Rusty complained, drawing their attention to him. In truth, they'd both forgotten he was still there. "I think I liked it better when you were fighting your feelings and being snarky. This lovey-dovey stuff makes me want to throw up."

"Then perhaps you should go to the beach bar and pick up your own woman for the evening," Gray suggested. "You might be less annoyed with us if you have something else to focus on."

"I think that sounds like a grand idea."

"Just grab my suitcase before you go," Gray ordered. "I can't carry it and Hali to the villa."

Hali shook her head. "I can walk."

"And yet I'm going to carry you," Gray insisted. "Your hip hurts. I know it does. We're going to do things my way for right now. You can have your way when we get back to the villa."

"Fine." Hali let loose an exasperated sigh. "I hate it when you're bossy though."

"You'll get used to it."

"Don't count on it."

"I guess we'll just have to wait and see."

SEVEN

"Thanks for doing this," Gray said to Rusty when they were back at the villa. His brother showed no signs of leaving, so Gray provided him with a beer on the back patio so they could talk in private. "I know you have other things to do. Once the body showed up on the beach though..." He trailed off.

"You wanted to keep your witch safe," Rusty finished. "I get it." A small smile played at the corners of his mouth. "You're gone for her."

Gray squirmed uncomfortably and held up his hands. "I don't know what you want me to say."

"You could admit it. That will make torturing you easier." Rusty's grin was wolfish.

"You're going to torture me regardless."

"I am, but the more ammunition, the better."

Gray didn't have to consider it long. "I'm gone for her."

"I knew it." Rusty leaned back on the chair and fixed his brother with a smug look. "You know she's not like a pack female, right?" he asked after several seconds.

"I believe that's one of her primary selling points."

"No, I get it. The thing is, she's not going to kowtow to you because you're a man."

"I don't want her to kowtow to me."

"Then you'd better take it down a notch." Rusty turned serious now. "You're used to the men calling the shots in the pack. You don't necessarily believe that's the right way to go, but that's what we're used to. Your girlfriend is used to calling the shots for herself. She's not going to take kindly to your alpha thing springing up on the regular."

Gray placed his beer on the end table and rubbed his forehead. "I know. I keep telling myself that. I really don't want to boss her around."

"You just can't help yourself."

"I just can't help myself," Gray acknowledged. "When she's in pain, I feel it here." He tapped the spot above his heart. "I feel sick to my stomach and want to keep her from hurting."

"The hip," Rusty surmised. "What's the deal with that?"

Gray hesitated. It wasn't in his nature to talk out of turn. Hali was open about her injury, but he didn't want to trample on her boundaries. "She was injured. There's a surgery, but no guarantee it will fix everything. She's afraid of the surgery."

"It must be hard for her." Rusty took a pull on his beer. "She's a strong woman. Like ... really strong. It's a turn-on, quite frankly. If you hadn't spotted her first, I would be all over her."

Gray made a growling sound, which only served to make Rusty smile wider.

"It's okay, man," Rusty assured him. "I'm not moving on your woman. It wouldn't matter if I did anyway. She only has eyes for you, which is dumbfounding because I'm clearly the hotter brother."

Gray's eye roll was pronounced. "If you say so."

Rusty chuckled before sobering. "Tell me about the

merrow thing. Are they a threat? Because if they are, I can try to position some soldiers out here to serve as backup."

"You're going to position pack members out here?" Gray challenged. "There's no way. I'm the enemy as far as they're concerned."

"Not everybody thinks that." Rusty lowered his voice. "The older pack members don't like what you did in going up against an elder. The younger ones, though, don't like the antiquated ways that include marrying young females off to decrepit elders. You have more support than you realize for stepping in the way that you did."

"That won't help me now." Gray was firm. "Besides, I don't think Hali would like it if her territory was usurped by shifters. I don't know exactly how dangerous the merrow are. So far, they've just dropped a few threats. They haven't proven to be a physical threat. At least not yet."

"How long do you think that will last?"

"I don't know." The sound of shuffling feet on pavement drew Gray's attention to the side gate, where a lurching flamingo was making his appearance known. He glared at the sight of Wayne, Hali's familiar, who offered nothing of substance to their relationship as far as he could tell.

"Pardon me," Wayne slurred when he saw them. "May I be of service?" He tried to stand on one leg but fell against the couch.

"What's that?" Rusty demanded, his wide eyes signifying a mixture of confusion and delight.

"That would be Wayne," Gray replied dryly. "He's Hali's familiar."

"Like ... he's magical?" Rusty leaned forward so he could better watch Wayne try to right himself.

"I've yet to see him do anything magical other than put away fifteen beers in a night," Gray replied darkly.

"I can drink way more than that," Wayne shot back as he

made his way to the bed that had been set up in the corner of the patio. He was used to sleeping inside the villa—or sometimes on the beach or in the middle of the parking lot depending on where he passed out—but Gray had put his foot down weeks ago. Until he cleaned up his act, Wayne wasn't allowed inside. There had been a Cold War brewing between them ever since.

"Great," Gray drawled. "How about you go to sleep for now, huh?"

"Whatever." Wayne fell again on his way to the bed. He didn't bother adjusting to be more comfortable. Instead, he merely closed his eyes and instantly started snoring.

"Well, that is awesome," Rusty said on a laugh as he regarded the flamingo with something akin to wonder. "Who doesn't want a drunk flamingo sidekick?"

Gray raised his hand. "He's a pain, but Hali feels she has to keep him around because her grandmother assigned him to her."

"And her grandmother is head of the coven, right?"

Gray nodded. "Yeah. I'm thinking of trying to get a meeting with her after this trivia thing is over with."

Rusty's eyebrows hopped in surprise. "Why? Do you hate the flamingo that much?"

"I can't stand him," Gray acknowledged. "That's not why though. I see Wayne once a day at most. Sometimes not even that. He spends his time hitting up the tourists for snacks and cocktails. I figure he'll eventually work things out himself."

"Or die," Rusty agreed. "What do you want to see the grandmother about if not the bird?"

Gray hesitated, glancing over his shoulder to see if there was any movement in the windows of the villa. He knew Hali was inside. It wasn't her nature to eavesdrop on him and his brother, but he wanted to make sure. "Do you know anything about shamans?" he asked when he turned back.

Rusty shook his head. "Only what I've read here and there. Why?"

"Because it was brought to my attention earlier that we live in a magical world."

"Wow," Rusty deadpanned. "I'm so glad you finally figured that out. Things might've gotten embarrassing otherwise."

Gray ignored him. "Hali is afraid of the surgery. I hate that she's always in pain. If we could find the right shaman though..." He didn't finish what he was going to say. He didn't have to.

Realization dawned on Rusty's face. "I'll ask around," he said as he finished off his beer and stood. "That's a really great idea. I'm not sure if there's anybody in the area, but even if there's not, I bet I know where you could find someone."

Gray cocked his head, intrigue gripping his insides. "Where?"

"New Orleans. It's supposedly brimming with shamans. I'll make some calls and get back to you."

Gray stood so he was at eye level with his brother. "Thanks. I just can't stand when she's in pain. She's so stubborn, she's willing to put up with the pain rather than admit she might need help. I just want her to be happy and healthy."

"Aw." Rusty grabbed Gray's cheek and gave it a jiggle, earning a growl for his efforts. "You're so cute with her. I think she might be the one."

Two months ago, Gray would've laughed his brother right off the patio. Now, though, he didn't bother trying. "I know she's the one."

A momentary surge of delight flitted through Rusty's eyes. "I'm glad." He meant it. "You've been alone too long, and only because you did the right thing. If she's your match —and I hope she is because I really like her—then you have my support."

"She's my match," Gray confirmed. "I've felt it since the moment I saw her. Sure, I fought it, but I don't want to fight it any longer. She's amazing. I want to keep moving forward, not looking back."

"Oh, that's poetic," Rusty teased.

"Don't make me hurt you."

"Yeah, the teasing isn't going anywhere. As for the shaman, give me a few days. I think that's entirely doable."

That was exactly what Gray wanted to hear.

HALI ENJOYED WAKING UP TO GRAY IN her bed. Before they started spending their nights together, she often slept diagonally on her king-size bed and made no bones about it. She adjusted way quicker to sharing than she thought she would, and even though she was a big fan of a cool room when it was time to go down for the night, there was something about cuddling up against his big frame that made her feel warm all over.

This morning was no exception.

"Hey," she murmured when she realized he was already awake and checking his phone. "Problem?"

"Not as far as I can tell," he replied, dropping a kiss on her wrinkled brow. "I wanted to make sure Dominic didn't run wild down the strip last night and get himself into trouble. As far as I can tell, he was quiet."

"That's good, right?"

"It's better than the alternative." Gray dropped his phone on the nightstand and wrapped both of his arms around Hali's slim frame so he could cuddle with her for a few minutes. "How did you sleep?"

"Pretty good, all things considered."

He didn't appreciate the caveat. "Meaning what?"

"Meaning I might have dreamed about the merrow."

His fingers were gentle as he brushed her dark hair back from her face, his gaze searching. "Do you want to talk about it?"

"There's not much to talk about," Hali replied. "I was on the beach. He was following me. It was like a scene from a horror movie. He didn't say anything. He didn't catch me. It honestly wasn't a big deal."

"It sounds like an anxiety dream."

"And yet I'm not feeling very anxious." She rubbed her nose against his cheek. "You don't have to worry about me," she said after several seconds. "I'm perfectly fine."

"I can't help it. In case you haven't noticed, I'm kind of fond of you."

"Oh, I've noticed." She gave him a soft kiss. "Is that what you were talking about with your brother last night?"

Gray felt put on the spot. He refused to lie to her—that was not the foundation he wanted to build their relationship on—but he wasn't ready to talk to her about the shaman yet either. He didn't want to get her hopes up if it wasn't an option. "He got to meet Wayne last night," he explained, frowning at the memory. "I seriously hate that stupid bird."

"Join the club." Hali wrinkled her nose. "I'm stuck with him for now though. My grandmother says that he's important to my development as a witch. I haven't figured out how, but she's rarely wrong. Now that he's sleeping outside, I barely notice him."

"I doubt he's going to keep from bothering you over the long haul."

"Maybe not, but he's not a concern for right now."

"What is a concern for right now?"

"I was thinking we could go to the restaurant out on the beach and have breakfast. They're going to start setting up for the trivia contest today, and that will be a good vantage point."

"Because you think the murder really did have something to do with the trivia contest," Gray surmised.

"Do you believe otherwise?"

He hesitated and then shook his head. "No. I know we have no proof that the contest and the murder are connected, but I feel in my gut that they are."

"So, maybe checking out the setup of the contest—especially since you've been hired to protect one of the highest profile participants—is a good idea."

Gray agreed, his fingers digging into her sides as he began to tickle her. "I have another good idea though. I think we should do my idea first because it involves this bed. Then we can do your idea after."

"I can probably be persuaded to go that route," Hali said on a giggle. "You're going to have to lay out your idea in great detail for me though. You know, just so I have a clear picture of what you have in mind."

"Oh, see, that's exactly what I want to do." His mouth descended on hers. "Get ready, because this is the best idea I've ever had."

HALI AND GRAY WERE BOTH HAPPY AND glowing when they made their way to the beach restaurant. The menu was the same as their normal morning haunt, but without air conditioning, the temperature was nowhere near as comfortable.

"I can see why we don't come here more often," Gray grumbled as he settled to the best of his ability across from her. "I'm going to sweat through this shirt before we're done eating."

"It's okay when the breeze kicks off the Gulf," Hali countered. She leaned over the table and rested her hand on his forearm, pulsing a small bit of magic into him and filling his features with wonder.

"What did you just do?" he asked, staring at his arm. "Why am I suddenly so much more comfortable?"

"It's just a little spell I've been working on since I was a teenager and found out that I'm not a big fan of sweating," Hali replied. "It will last about an hour. You won't sweat through your shirt and will be able to focus on your food for the duration without being uncomfortable."

"Well, that's awesome." He touched his forehead, checking for sweat. "How come you don't use this spell more often? We've sweated together on the beach more times than I can count."

Hali shot him an amused look. "Are you complaining about sweating with me on the beach?"

"No, I'm just confused."

"It's not healthy to eradicate the sweating process entirely. You need to sweat. I just don't find it necessary to sweat during meals."

"Ah." He nodded in understanding. "I get it."

They ceased conversation long enough to give their orders to a server Gray didn't recognize. Once their juice and coffee were delivered, they turned their attention to the activity on the beach. An entire team was present to build the trivia stage, and they were fascinated as they watched the work commence.

"You've never mentioned if you're a fan of trivia," Gray noted as he leaned back in his chair, long legs stretched out in front of him.

"I know a lot of useless factoids, if that's what you're asking," she teased. "If I'm going to compete, however, there's got to be more than movie knowledge on the line."

He nodded in understanding. "You'll be rooting for Lana, right?"

"She could really use the win for her self-esteem," Hali

agreed. "She's the type of person who only relaxes when she feels comfortable with a subject. Unfortunately for her, I've never actually seen her get comfortable. I'm kind of hoping she'll realize this competition is her natural habitat and adjust accordingly."

"You have a good heart."

The statement, however simple, threw Hali. "It's just an observation."

"No, you're good with your regulars," he insisted. "You treat them as if they're family, not customers. That's why they're loyal to you, because you really do care about them."

"Lana doesn't have a mean bone in her body," Hali supplied. "She's a good person. Sure, she's socially awkward, but we're all socially awkward in our way. Her fun facts are simply a way for her to communicate."

"And because she's a good person, you play the game," Gray mused.

"I don't ever want anyone to feel out of place," she replied. "I get annoyed with people as much as the next person, but I've never much understood the need to make yourself feel big by making others small."

"Aw, see, that's one of the reasons I've got it bad for you." Gray took her arm and pressed a kiss to the spot on the inside of her wrist. "That's another thing I talked about with Rusty last night."

Amusement washed over Hali's makeup-free features. She didn't bother with makeup when she knew she was just going to sweat it off over the course of the day. "You talked about how bad you have it for me?"

He nodded. "Rusty seems to think it's cute. He believes I've found my tribe."

Because Gray didn't often want to talk about his past with the pack, Hali hesitated before speaking. She knew they would have to be comfortable with all subjects if they wanted to make this work over the long haul, so she ultimately barreled forward. "Do you miss your old tribe?"

Gray cocked his head, considering, and then lifted one shoulder. "I guess I miss knowing how things were supposed to go for me. It's more like I believe I should be missing them. When I look at you, though, I don't miss anything. In fact, I'm glad to have the past in the past because I don't want pack politics clouding my future."

"What if they were to invite you back in though?" Hali asked in a soft voice. "Would you go?"

"I don't know. Probably not. The thing is, I wouldn't mind being able to see some of my old friends. I would enjoy being able to hang out with my brother and not have to worry if anybody sees us. I might even like seeing my parents again, although that's an iffy proposition.

"I wouldn't give up this life or spending time with you for anything though," he continued. "I was never built for pack life. I miss some of the people, but the rigidity—the hierarchy —they're things I will never miss."

It was exactly what Hali wanted to hear. "If I can help you in any way on that front, just tell me, okay? I want to be the person who makes you feel better, not worse."

"You could never make me feel worse."

"That's a bold statement, but we both know it's not true." She was matter of fact. "We're both alphas in our own way. There are times we're going to have to tread lightly with one another."

He already knew that and nodded. "There are. Just know, I don't really want to be a bossy monster. Sometimes I can't help myself."

"I know. I'm the same way. I don't want to be a nag."

"So, we'll just do our best." He linked his fingers with hers. "I want you to be more than my girlfriend. You're my partner in this as well. We're still figuring things out, but I have faith we'll manage it."

Hali nodded. "I feel the same way."

"Good. Now, let's watch what they're doing here. I have no idea if it will be helpful or not, but I find the entire thing fascinating."

"Funnily enough, I was just thinking the same thing."

EIGHT

Gray knocked eight times before Dominic answered the door. The trivia guru was shirtless, in nothing more than a pair of boxer shorts, and he looked disgruntled with life.

"I was about to call security to open the door for me," Gray snapped. He didn't feel it was prudent to mention Cecily had provided him with a key before it was absolutely necessary. "Why are you sleeping so late?"

Dominic shot Gray a dirty look and then turned on his heel to pad to the kitchen. "I didn't realize I'd inherited a new father. Now that I know, please continue with the harassment."

Even though he was annoyed, Gray tempered his response. Fueling antagonism wouldn't suit him well for this job. "I'm sorry. I was worried. You went to bed at eleven o'clock. I was just concerned."

Dominic turned on the Keurig and rooted through the available pods without glancing over his shoulder. "I went to my room at eleven," he countered. "I got bored after fifteen minutes of television, however, and went to the lobby bar to pick up a woman."

Gray's heart sank. "Is she still here?"

"Nope. She left about two hours ago, at which point I continued sleeping. It was a long night." His grin was impish when he swiveled. "She had pretty good stamina, which is a relief, because you wouldn't believe how many duds I've picked up in lobby bars."

Gray didn't know whether he should shake Dominic or punch him. "That's a great way to talk about women."

"Oh, just because you found the one jewel in this tarnished crown, that doesn't mean you've earned the right to judge me," Dominic admonished. "I was bored. I needed something to take the edge off. Since preliminary rounds start today for the contest, I figured sex was a better vice to indulge in than alcohol."

"Well, at least you're honest." Gray hopped onto one of the counter stools and flicked his gaze to the grand view of the Gulf. "It's a nice day. You should get dressed. Cecily provided me with an itinerary, and you need to be down on the beach in two hours."

Dominic let loose a haphazard wave. "It's fine. They won't start without me. I'm too important."

"At least your ego isn't out of control or anything," Gray muttered.

"I happen to think a healthy ego is one of my better traits." Dominic shoved a mug under the opening before turning to face Gray. "How was your night with your pretty witch? Was it down and dirty or light and pretty? I can see her going either way."

Gray managed to keep from snarling, but it wasn't easy. "We should talk about the ground rules going forward."

"I don't happen to believe rules apply to me."

"Well, they do." Gray was having none of the man's lip.

"First up, if you're going to be wandering around late at night, you need to text me your whereabouts."

"Why? Would you have come back to babysit me if you'd known?"

It was a fair question, and one Gray wasn't certain he had an answer for. "I just prefer knowing. Leave the decision-making on stuff like that up to me."

"See, I'm not sure I can allow you to be my wingman when I'm looking for women," Dominic argued. "You're a good-looking guy. Even though you wouldn't look twice at my prospects because of that pretty witch, that doesn't mean they wouldn't be distracted by you."

"I thought you had cupid powers in your arsenal," Gray argued. "Doesn't that mean you don't need to worry about stuff like that?"

"One would think, but attraction—especially when alcohol is involved—is a fickle beast. Because people aren't always rational when drunk, that means they can't be easily controlled. Sometimes it's easy. Sometimes it isn't. I don't want to be in competition with my own bodyguard."

"You're not in competition with me," Gray assured him. "I don't want to play the game."

"Because of Hali?" Dominic waggled his eyebrows suggestively.

"Listen, she's going to be the second ground rule." Gray's tone was no nonsense. "Hali is very important to me. You're not to mess with her. You're also not to ask inappropriate questions about her."

"Define inappropriate."

"You know exactly what I'm talking about," Gray snapped. "You're being a tool. Hali doesn't deserve whatever innuendo you're trying to throw at her. It's unfair, and I'm not just going to sit back and allow it."

Dominic took a moment to consider Gray's words. He

collected his mug of coffee, sipped, then smiled on an easy chuckle. "You're kind of weird with that witch. Like ... over-the-top weird. I guess I get it though. She's a catch. Just know, I'm not actually trying to be inappropriate. I'm simply curious. You two are an odd mix that seems to somehow fit together perfectly. You have no idea how rare that is."

"Hali is a force to be reckoned with," Gray acknowledged. "I won't tolerate disrespect."

"Dude, she might be hot, but she's way above my pay grade. I need a woman who is simple and doesn't want to delve deep on anything, including emotions or feelings. That means your witch is out of my league."

"My witch is most definitely out of your league."

"I'm curious for your sake," Dominic continued. "You're a glum guy except when she's around. I want to see how happy you can be."

Gray thought about waking up with Hali, how soft she was in his arms, how he couldn't stop smiling when they were together. "Don't worry about me," he insisted after several seconds. "I've got everything under control in my life. Let's focus on you, huh?"

"I am my favorite subject," Dominic agreed.

"Somehow that doesn't surprise me."

LANA WAS ALL AFLUTTER AS SHE SAT at the Salty Cauldron and waited for her name to be called for the second preliminary round. She clapped her hands around a cup of iced tea, but despite the woman's determination to put on a confident front, Hali didn't miss the fact that she was clearly nervous.

"Your hands are shaking." Hali wrapped her hands around Lana's hands and then added a bit of magic to the mix. It wasn't much—not enough to be considered cheating—but

Hali felt a self-esteem boost was in order, and she was gratified to find Lana's fingers immediately stopped shaking in the aftermath.

"I'm nervous," Lana admitted sheepishly.

"You've participated in trivia tournaments before," Hali argued as she moved away and grabbed several oranges to chop for garnishes. "Just think of this tournament like you would those tournaments."

"That's easier said than done," Lana argued. "All the other tournaments I've participated in have been a quarter of the size of this one. It's freaky to think about, but I can't help it. If I win and make it to the actual tournament—the finale I mean —I could be on television."

"And that frightens you?" Hali queried.

"It's just a lot of pressure. I don't do well under pressure."

Hali let loose a sigh and rested on her elbows as she leaned in. Various people milled around the bar, but Lana was the one who needed her most. That meant Hali would be there for her, no matter what. "Give me some fun facts," she instructed.

"You want fun facts?" Lana seemed surprised.

"It will relax you and I do love hearing your fun facts."

"Okay." Lana licked her lips. "In some parts of Texas, it's illegal to swear in front of a dead person."

Hali considered it for a beat. "I can see that. It's Texas. Give me another one."

"A man once wore sixty shirts and nine pairs of jeans to the airport to avoid extra fees."

Hali choked on a laugh as she pictured the security guard's face when he saw that many outfits on one man. "That sounds delightful. Keep going."

"Dolly Parton once lost a Dolly Parton look-alike competition."

Hali froze. "Seriously?"

Lana nodded solemnly. "Isn't that freaky?"

"Totally." Hali caught Gray's gaze as he cut toward the bar, Dominic on his heels. He didn't look happy. "Tell me more," she ordered Lana as she filled a cup with iced tea for her shifter boyfriend.

"Ninety percent of money has cocaine on it."

Gray arched an eyebrow as he grabbed his usual stool and leaned in for a kiss from Hali. "What are you guys doing?" he asked as he slid a look toward Lana.

"Lana is telling me fun facts," Hali replied. "She's a little nervous." She shot a warning look toward Dominic when a gleam appeared in his eye. "If you're going to make things worse for her, I'm going to make things worse for you."

Dominic made a protesting sound and mock-clutched at his heart. "I'm wounded. Do you think so little of me that you would suggest I would purposely sabotage my competition?"

"Don't push it," Hali warned. "What do you want to drink?"

"I'll have a bourbon and Coke," Dominic replied.

Hali made a face. "Don't you have to compete?"

"So?"

"So, you can't have bourbon if you're going to compete. You can have some iced tea."

"Man, this is a rough bar," Dominic complained. "And to think I thought the whole point of a place like this was to order what you want."

"Yes, well, you are kind of an idiot," Hali agreed on a grin as she slid the iced tea in front of him. "Throw some more fun facts at me, Lana. I want to hear them."

Lana wasted a dubious look on Dominic but continued as instructed. Reciting facts was cathartic to her, something Hali knew well. "People have tried to sue God," she offered. "For negligence, failure to keep people away from the devil, and even natural disasters."

"That seems like a rough gig," Gray noted.

"Also, Uranus was first named George," Lana volunteered, clearly warming to the responses she was getting. "William Herschel first discovered the planet in 1781 and named it Georgium Sidus in honor of King George III."

Hali couldn't stifle her laugh. "George."

"If you edit all the quiet staring in the *Twilight* films together, there's twenty-six minutes of intense silence between the five films."

"That's just disturbing," Gray commented.

Lana, losing interest in them, began reciting fun facts to herself. "Peanuts are used to make dynamite."

Hali kept her concerned gaze on Lana for a beat longer and then focused on Gray. "How has the rest of your morning been?"

"Well, my client did not go to bed as promised last night," he replied. "Instead, he went down to the lobby bar, picked up a woman with surprising stamina, and got his rocks off. He was grumpy when I woke him up this morning."

"That sounds ... lovely."

"I'm right here," Dominic complained. "You can't talk about me when I'm right here."

As if on cue, a voice echoed off the beach, telling contestants that the second preliminary round was set to begin.

"That's me," Lana announced as she hopped off the stool. She stopped long enough to finish the rest of her iced tea and then shot two thumbs-up toward Hali. "I've got this."

"You do," Hali encouraged softly. "You're going to be fine. Just remember to breathe."

"Yeah. The house from the original *Texas Chainsaw Massacre* movie is now a family restaurant."

"Yes, because who wouldn't want to eat there?" Gray teased, offering up a salute to Lana as she scampered across the beach.

Dominic was slower to follow.

"Don't torture her," Hali warned. "I'll torture you if you do."

"Now I get what you see in her," Dominic drawled to Gray. "Who doesn't love a woman who threatens bodily harm over a trivia game?"

"Do as she says," Gray replied. "If you're going to torture someone, it had better not be Lana."

"I make no promises."

Hali narrowed her eyes.

"Except that I'll leave your friend alone," Dominic added. "I've got this. You don't have to worry."

"Keep it that way," Hali said stonily.

EVEN THOUGH HALI THOUGHT HERSELF ambivalent to trivia contests, she found herself watching the second preliminary round with rapt attention. As she'd predicted, Lana was nervous for several minutes, but after getting her first question right, she settled into a routine. She was better than almost everybody else playing alongside her. The only one who even came close to her level of knowledge was Dominic, and Hali could see why he was considered a rock star on the tournament circuit.

"He's good, huh?" a woman in a trivia shirt asked as she settled at Hali's bar.

"Hmm?" Hali dragged her eyes from what was happening on the beach and focused on the woman. She wore a lanyard identifying herself as Mia Jankowski, assistant tournament coordinator. She had what looked to be a lot of hair pulled back in a neat bun, and her face was red from something other than exertion.

"Are you a northerner?" Hali asked sympathetically as she took in the woman's sweating features.

"What gave it away?" Mia used a napkin to mop at the sweat on her face. "Doesn't this look like my natural habitat?"

Hali chuckled and moved to the ice bin. She grabbed a baggie from the counter and filled it with ice before sealing it. "I know this is going to sound weird, but press it to your lower back, not your face. It will cool you down."

Mia looked dubious but game at the same time and did as instructed. "Oh, that feels amazing," she said on a reverent whisper once she adjusted to the cold on her back.

"Keep it there for at least five minutes," Hali instructed. "Trust me. That's how the locals survive summer here."

"I can't even imagine." Mia closed her eyes. "I haven't felt this good in hours. Can I have a lemonade to finish the perfection?"

"Absolutely." Hali filled a cup and placed it in front of the tournament coordinator. "Do you travel all over the country with these guys?"

"Unfortunately." Mia's expression was sour when she opened her eyes again. "I prefer when the tournaments are in a climate-controlled environment if you want to know the truth. I thought the time we had the tournament outside in Salem was the absolute worst. It was windy and cold. This is actually worse than that though."

"You'll adjust," Hali assured her. "They've got big fans pointed at the contestants, so they're fine. Dominic doesn't even look like he's sweating."

Mia spared a cursory glance over her shoulder and scowled. "You have to be human to sweat, and he's not human."

Her interest piqued, Hali darted a look toward Gray, who had positioned himself close to the fans so he could remain cool and still keep an eye on Dominic. He didn't look in her direction. "You don't like Dominic?" she prodded finally.

"Nobody likes Dominic. He's a tool. He always tries to be

the biggest story at every tournament because he's hungry for attention."

"Do you think he'll do the same at this tournament?"

Mia offered up a one-shoulder shrug. "I have no idea. I think it's going to be hard to overshadow what happened to Brian."

Here was her opening, Hali realized. She'd been looking for a way to get more information on the dead guy, and it had just fallen into her lap. "Yeah, that's quite the tragedy," she acknowledged. "Did they tell you anything about that?"

"No. We just know he was stabbed. The cops aren't saying anything."

"What did he even do for you guys?"

"He handled the trivia bundles."

Hali was at a loss. "I don't know what that means," she admitted after a beat.

"Oh, all the questions are sorted into different bundles. There's usually one bundle per round. It was Brian's job to organize all that."

"That seems like a high-pressure job." Hali considered it for several seconds. "Did anything change because of his murder?"

"Oh, no." Mia shook her head. "All the bundles were locked in the hotel safe before he died. Even if someone wanted to get their hands on those bundles, there are better ways to do it than murder someone. It's not as if Brian walked around with them."

"So, you don't think he died because of his connection to the tournament," Hali prodded.

"Definitely not. Why? What have you heard?"

"Nothing," Hali replied hurriedly. "I haven't heard anything. That's why I was asking questions. Everybody here is aflutter. I was hoping that they'd told you something."

"Unfortunately, as far as I can tell, they're not going to

share anything with us," Mia replied. "Brian was a nice guy. He didn't pick the questions though. They're computer generated. He just separated the questions into bundles and locked them up. That was the entirety of his job."

"So, even if someone had wanted control of the questions, killing Brian would have no bearing on what was asked," Hali mused.

"Pretty much. This is a fine-tuned machine. There are protocols in place." She sipped her lemonade. "Just out of curiosity, do you think Brian was killed because of the tournament? Like, do you have a lot of murders here?"

"Not really," Hali replied. "People die of course—that happens everywhere—but we don't see a lot of deaths around the resort. It's not like Miami. We're not considered a violent city."

"Right." Mia bobbed her head. "Ah, well," she said after a beat. "It's a tragedy all around. I hope they find who did it. The tournament must go on though." She finished draining her drink and got to her feet. "Do you mind if I take the bag of ice with me?" she asked hopefully.

"Knock yourself out." Hali kept her smile in place even though she didn't believe there was much to be happy about. "If you need a refill, you know where to find me."

"Thanks so much for this." She gestured with her free hand toward the baggie she was holding to her back. "I thought I was going to seriously die here a few minutes ago. You're a lifesaver."

"I aim to please."

"Well, you didn't miss with me. I'm sure I'll be seeing you around."

"I'm sure you will too."

NINE

The tiki bar was hopping during the trivia contest, but very few people stayed out to drink once the rounds were finished. That meant Hali wasn't nearly as busy as she expected.

"They have a dinner over at the main restaurant tonight," Gray explained as he watched Dominic schmooze an eliminated contestant. The girl—because if she was older than twenty-one Gray would eat his own hand—was in tears, and Dominic was rubbing her back while cooing words of encouragement. "I don't think you're going to be busy."

"Probably not," Hali agreed as she followed Gray's gaze. "Do you want me to go over there and save that girl?"

The question threw Gray. "Do you want to go over there and save that girl?"

Hali held out her hands. "She's not a child. She's an adult. You have to be eighteen to participate, and I know they were checking IDs."

"That doesn't mean she deserves to be played."

"No, but we don't know she *is* being played." Hali opted to be reasonable. "She could be playing him."

"Or they could be playing each other," Gray rationalized. "I get it. She just looks so young and vulnerable."

"You have a white knight complex," Hali noted as she untied her apron and shoved it under the counter. "You want to save people. It's who you are."

He slowly slid his eyes to her. "Is there a warning in there?"

Hali shook her head. "I might give you grief if I didn't recognize the tendency in myself. We both like to save people. The good news is, I happen to believe we're both going to be in the position where we get to save each other regularly going forward. I'm not sure that girl—she's a young woman actually —needs to be saved though. He's not being a complete and total jerk or anything."

"Yet," Gray clarified. "He's not being a leech *yet*."

"Well ... that brings me back to my original question. Do you want me to go over there and intervene?"

Gray considered it for several seconds and then shook his head. "No. That's not necessary. She's in charge of her own life. It's not as if he's exerting undue control over her. She's a big girl."

"Good boy." Hali patted his arm. "And because you went against your baser urges and opted for the sensible route, how about I knock off early and buy you dinner?"

Now Gray was surprised for a different reason. "Since when do you knock off early in the middle of the week?"

"As you pointed out, the bar is dead. I've got two other bartenders on. They can close it down. I have a few things to discuss with you anyway, and I think it would sound better over pasta."

"Ooh, the Italian restaurant." Gray perked up. He was a big fan of the seafood risotto at the resort's lauded Italian spot. "That sounds pretty good to me."

"I thought you would like that." Hali took the time to tell

her bartenders where she was going. They waved her off. By the time they were heading down the sidewalk toward the resort's main building, Dominic and his new friend had disappeared. "Where did they go?" she asked when she found Gray studying their route with intense eyes.

"That way." He pointed in the direction they were already heading. "I heard them mention that there's a meal for contestants at the main restaurant, but the bigwigs are eating at the same place we are."

Hali already knew that but feigned ignorance. "Fancy that."

"Don't even." Gray poked her side before taking her hand. "How come you want to spy on the tournament organizers?"

Hali lifted one shoulder in a shrug. "I heard something from one of the event coordinators today. She has no love for Dominic by the way. She called him a tool."

"That can't be the first time someone has used that word to describe him. You can't be surprised."

"Nope." Hali shook her head. "What was a surprise is that the dead guy was in charge of the question bundles. She didn't seem to think that was important information."

"But you do," Gray surmised. "I'm intrigued myself. Although, I'm not certain I know what question bundles are."

"According to Mia—that was her name—a computer decides on the questions for each round. Then it spits them out in digital and hard copies. The hard copies for this tournament have already been locked in the resort safe. Mia said that no matter what happened, there was no messing with the questions."

"But you believe otherwise."

"Let's just say I'm not one to believe that anything is truly safe," Hali replied. "I also don't believe that the bundle guy was picked at random. It feels off to me."

"Ah, my curious little witch does love a mystery," he teased.

"Like you don't."

"I'm definitely curious," he agreed. "What do you think the bigwigs are going to tell you though?"

"I don't know if they're going to tell us anything. It can't do any harm to give it a try though. It's not as if you have to choke down the food because it's too good. There will be no suffering."

"No, and it's quiet and romantic." He squeezed her hand. "Any sign of the others today?" he asked after a beat.

Hali didn't have to ask who he was referring to. "Nope. I haven't even felt an inkling of them. I'm guessing that they wouldn't want to hang around this many people if they can help it."

"I wouldn't assume that."

"I won't make a mistake because I overlook anything," Hali promised. "It's just a feeling anyway. I don't expect them to move during the tournament. There are too many people around to bear witness to an attack. They haven't survived this long by making mistakes either."

"Good point." Gray released her hand and slid his arm around her waist. "I just want you to be careful."

"You're going to be careful too, right?"

"Always."

"Then I guess we have that in common."

IT DIDN'T TAKE HALI LONG TO PINPOINT WHERE the tournament bigwigs had been seated. She requested a table not too far away, but not so close it would be obvious she was eavesdropping. In deference to Gray, she went light on the garlic in case they wanted to embrace the romance later. Unfortunately for her, no matter how much she strained, she couldn't make out as much of the conversation as she would've liked. Gray's super hearing was a different story, however. He could make out everything, although he seemed confused by what he was hearing.

"They think it was a random mugging," he said in a low voice.

Hali frowned. "How much money could he have possibly been carrying?"

"I don't think they consider stuff like that," Gray replied. "It's easier for them to assume it's not connected to his position with the tournament. If it is connected, that means they have to look at themselves ... and I'm willing to guarantee that's something they don't want to consider."

"It's still stupid." Hali pushed back her empty plate and smiled at the incoming server. "The food was great as usual, Gina," she said to the bubbly blonde. "I wish I could roll around naked in the marinara sauce."

Gray raised a flirty eyebrow. "Would you be alone for this endeavor?"

Gina laughed and shook her head. "It's a pretty basic sauce. I think that's why it's so good. Do you guys want dessert?"

Hali slid her eyes toward Gray, but he shook his head. "Unfortunately, I think we're full," she said. "I would suggest throwing some tiramisu in a box for later, but I think we might take a walk on the beach before bed. It's a nice night."

"Just don't go down to the beach bar," Gina replied. "I hear that's where the contestants are going. That tool Dominic—the one who everybody is oohing and aahing about —has riled them all up to do shots."

Gray shifted on his chair. "How do you know that?"

"The gossip mill here at the resort is a well-oiled machine," Hali replied. "The servers from the main restaurant share the same break room as all the other restaurants."

"Yeah, Kelly was in there five minutes ago," Gina agreed. "She said that Dominic guy is an attention-seeking twit. Everybody is following him down to the beach bar though."

Hali studied Gray's profile, making note of the muscle working in his jaw, and then sighed. "Thanks for the tip, Gina. Can you just apply the bill to my villa?"

"Absolutely." Gina moved to the table of bigwigs next, leaving Hali to make things easier for Gray.

"I really should stop in and see Carrie," she said. "I didn't get much time to hang out with her yesterday after the body discovery. She claims I'm ignoring her in favor of you. I don't want to be *that* woman."

Gray shot her a grateful look. "I just want to look in on him and make sure he's not causing trouble."

"And I want to see Carrie," Hali said. "It looks like our interests overlap." She reached into her pocket to grab some cash for a tip, but Gray stopped her.

"You paid for dinner," he admonished. "I think it's only fair that I handle the tip."

"Technically, I don't pay when we eat on resort grounds," she reminded him. "I just get a monthly tally from Franklin, so I can see exactly how much he's seemingly paying me for my silence."

"I hate it when you put it that way." Gray threw two twenties on the table and stood. "I still want to punch that guy whenever I think about what happened to you."

"I survived," she reminded him. "Not only that, but I got an awesome tiki bar and a place to live out of the deal."

And chronic pain, Gray silently added. He knew darned well she would trade the bar and villa if it meant she wasn't constantly fighting to remain upright at the end of her shifts sometimes. "We're going to agree to table this discussion." He made up his mind on the spot. "It makes me mad, and you trying to see the bright side of things even though he could've killed you makes me even angrier. I don't want to fight."

"I don't either," Hali assured him. "Especially since I'm convinced that seeing Dominic in action at the beach bar is going to make us want to fight for different reasons."

"Probably," Gray agreed. "Let's just not talk about Franklin tonight, huh?"

"That's always my motto."

THE NIGHT WASN'T OVERLY WARM AND THERE was a nice breeze for the walk. Gray and Hali held hands as they watched the water lap at the sand. On a different night, they might've shed their shoes and waded into the surf, shared kisses coming fast and furious between whispers. Tonight, they were both intent on the trek to the beach bar.

"Is that Wayne?" Gray asked when they were halfway to their destination, pointing toward a familiar figure about fifty feet in front of them. The flamingo, clearly drunk, appeared to be hitting on an egret.

"Yeah, that's him." Hali made a tsking sound. "He's a complete and total idiot. He seems to forget that not all birds are created equal when he's been drinking."

"Have you considered making him dry out?"

"Yes. Believe it or not, he's even more intolerable when sober than he is when drunk."

"That is really hard to picture. When was the last time he was sober?"

"About two months after I inherited him. He dried out for a full three weeks. Then he went from surly flamingo to Eeyore in training. Everything was terrible. There was no joy to be found in life. Sadly, I was glad he went back on the sauce, even though I know it's the worst possible thing for him."

"Have you considered talking to your grandmother?"

"She doesn't listen. She keeps saying there's a reason she assigned Wayne to me, and I'll just have to suffer until I figure out what that reason is."

"That seems unfair."

"Life isn't fair."

"No, I guess it's not." Gray watched her carefully to see if she was favoring her hip. For now, she seemed fine. He had a feeling he was going to have to sucker her into a piggyback ride for the trek back. That was Future Gray's problem, however. "You're beautiful," he announced out of nowhere, drinking in her ridiculously pretty profile in the moonlight. "Have I told you that today?"

It was dark, but Gray didn't miss the way Hali's cheeks flushed. "No, but thank you. I happen to think you're beautiful too."

"Oh, I know." He puffed out his chest. "According to Dominic, I'm good looking enough for him not to want me riding shotgun on his pickup trips."

Hali laughed, as she was certain he intended. "That sounds just about right."

"He drives me crazy," Gray acknowledged. "The thing is, I can't help feeling there's something more beneath the surface."

"Like what?"

"I'm not sure. I just have this feeling."

"I get feelings too, and I'm right there with you. We'll just have to keep our eyes open."

"That's the plan." Gray slowed his pace when a figure appeared on the beach in front of him. He immediately looked over his shoulder to make certain they weren't about to be boxed in, and then focused on the shadow. The closer they got, the more recognizable the figure became.

"Brandon," Gray said by way of greeting as they stopped in front of the lackadaisical beach denizen. Brandon Bigelow was a former classmate who now went by the name Bod and ruled a hippie cult on the beach. He wasn't a favorite friend by any stretch of the imagination, but Gray found him mostly harmless.

"Bod," he snapped. "My name is Bod. Why can't you remember that, *Grayson*?"

Gray made a face. He hated his given name. It sounded stuffy, which he had no doubt was the vibe his parents were going for when naming him. "I can't call you Bod. It's weird."

"It's God with a B. How is that weird?"

"You don't want me to answer that."

"Whatever." Bod shook his head and then smiled at Hali. His gaze almost immediately landed on their joined hands. "I take it you guys are no longer fighting the inevitable."

"Don't be weird," Gray warned.

Bod ignored him. "I always wanted you to join my ranks, Hali. Now I see you were destined for something different. I'm sad for myself but happy for my friend."

Hali's lips swished back and forth. She didn't know Bod nearly as well as Gray, but she'd always found him amusing. As far as cults were concerned, his Brotherhood of the Setting Sun was as innocuous as they came. The only things Hali had witnessed when in close proximity to them were rampant sex and marijuana usage. Nobody was treated poorly. Nobody was abused. Nobody was giving money they didn't have to give. It was basically unwashed Bohemians enjoying the beach.

"I'm sorry to have missed out on my window," she replied. "I think it was probably for the best though."

"Oh, most definitely," Bod agreed solemnly. "Your strong personality wouldn't mesh well with my mantra."

"You have a mantra?" Gray challenged. "Does it have something to do with your aversion to soap?" He waved his free hand in front of his face. "Seriously, dude, I know you want to embrace nature and all, but there's no crime against taking a shower."

"You wound me." Bod mock-clutched at his heart. "I'll have you know, I showered on Thursday. That was three days ago."

Gray did the math in his head. "That was six days ago."

"Really?" Bod looked momentarily perplexed. Then he offered up a shrug. "Time flies when you're having fun. What are you guys doing out here this evening? Are you looking for a bit of romance? If so, I have a special product for that."

"You have sex pot?" Hali demanded. "I didn't even know that was a thing."

"It's a flavored oil my people produce and sell."

"The oil is probably from their bodies," Gray interjected.

"That would explain the smell," Hali mused.

"Oh, it can't possibly be that bad." Bod lifted an arm and took a sniff. "I can't smell anything."

"That's not a ringing endorsement," Gray argued. "What are you even doing down here? You're usually on the opposite side of the resort. Did someone force you to move?"

"Actually, the buzz from all those people flooding the beach for that tournament down by the resort was messing with our vibe," Bod replied. "We're going to spend the weekend down here before returning to our normal grounds. We don't like the newbies."

Hali's interest was officially piqued. Bod might be a burnout, but he'd survived on the beach for a very long time because he was a master at reading people. "What don't you like about the newbies?"

"They smell like deception."

"And what does deception smell like?"

"Rotten eggs and Axe Body Spray."

Hali slid her eyes to Gray and found him grinning. "Is that an inside joke?" she asked.

"It's just Brandon being Brandon," he replied. "If I remember correctly, you were a big fan of Axe Body Spray back in the day. It's kind of ironic that you hate it now."

"That's how I recognize it for what it is," Bod replied solemnly. "I was a deceiver when I was younger. Your beach is flooded with them now. You should be careful."

Gray gripped Hali's hand tighter. "Have you heard something we should know about?"

"It's more of a feeling," Bod replied. "If I hear anything, though, you'll be the first to know."

"Thanks for that." Gray waited until they were past Bod—and the smell—to speak again. "Even he recognizes there's something funky going on here."

"Yeah." Hali nodded. "Let's check out the bar. If the contestants have been whispering about anything, Carrie will have heard it. At the very least, we can have a drink and watch them interact. We can still go to bed early if we choose."

"Not to sleep, right?"

"Of course not to sleep. We're responsible, not boring."

"Good to know."

TEN

The beach bar was attached to another resort, and the booming music shook the bridge that led from the sand to the deck bar as Hali and Gray started across. The facility boasted live music four nights a week, and it was a big draw, even though Hali could take or leave the bands.

"I can't believe Carrie works here," Gray groused as he scanned the area behind them to make sure nobody was following.

"She makes really good money," Hali replied. "I thought about asking her to work at my bar for a hot minute when I first took it over—I was in over my head—but we both agreed that was a bad idea for our friendship."

"You don't think you guys could survive you being her boss?"

Hali lifted one shoulder. "I don't think it's healthy for a relationship when one person is in a dominant position," she replied. "We've been equals our whole lives. I wouldn't have been any more comfortable bossing her around than she would've been taking orders. This is better ... although there are times when I picture how our days could've gone, gossiping between guests, and I'm a little sad."

"Well, I'm your partner this week." Gray squeezed her hand. "You can gossip with me."

"Sure." Hali bobbed her head, not missing a beat. "Did you hear that Sara Astor and John Butterfield are having an affair?"

Gray's forehead creased. "I don't know those people."

"And that's why I want Carrie to gossip with."

"Ah." Gray shifted Hali so she was in front of him when they walked onto the deck. "I see your point."

They stood at the entrance for several minutes, scanning the multiple levels of the deck. Ultimately, Hali recognized the blonde Dominic had been hitting on when he left the beach earlier, and they made their way in that direction.

The scene they found was of great interest to both of them. The trivia participants—even Lana—had taken over two rectangular tables side by side and seemed to be trying to one-up each other with fun facts.

"The Supreme Court has its own basketball court on the premises," David announced as he scanned faces imperiously. "It's called 'the highest court in the land'."

Only a few people applauded, which seemed to irritate him. He might've looked like a thumb, Hali mused, but he was clearly used to getting attention.

"It takes 364 licks to get to the center of a Tootsie Pop," Vinnie volunteered on a suggestive tongue thrust. "It's been studied."

Gray's hand landed on the center of Hali's back, his lips twitching.

Lana, much to Hali's surprise, entered the conversation next.

"The blob of toothpaste that sits on your toothbrush is called a nurdle," she said.

"Nurdle." Dominic burst out laughing as he leaned closer to the blonde. "That's awesome."

Lana beamed at him, and Hali felt a pang in her chest.

"It's okay," Gray assured her in a low voice. "Lana isn't his type. He won't take advantage of her."

Hali was going to make sure of that, but for now she let it go. "Let's find a table," she said.

"One that's not too far away." Gray agreed.

They settled at a small four-top about three tables over, and Hali was gratified when Carrie was the one who appeared next to take their order.

"I would like to think you're here to see me, but something tells me otherwise." Carrie's eyes darted to the trivia table. "Are you guys on babysitting duty?"

"Sort of," Hali replied. "Gray has been hired to watch the one in the middle over there." She pointed toward Dominic. "Apparently, he's a ladies' man and leaves a bevy of furious husbands in his wake."

Carrie made a face. "I can see that. He's got 'tool' written all over him. What do you guys want?"

"I'll have a Corona," Hali replied. She wanted to keep her alcohol consumption light in case there was an incident but feared they might draw attention if they were at a bar and not drinking.

"I'll have the same," Gray replied as he rested his hand on top of Hali's and stroked her fingers. "By the way, my brother has requested that I tell you he's still waiting for you to see the light."

"Aw, that's so sweet," Carrie replied. "If I leaned that way, I definitely might give him a shot. He's fun. Alas, he's lacking a few things—and we're talking important things—I need for a love match."

"I've told him." Gray grinned. "I promised I would put

some pressure on you though, and since he helped me last night, I felt obliged to follow through."

"That sounds like a story," Carrie noted. "I'm due for a break in about ten. I'll swing back around to hear it."

"That sounds good." Hali beamed at her. "Just out of curiosity, is this the only group of tournament participants you've seen this evening?" She inclined her head toward the raucous group in question.

"To my knowledge," Carrie confirmed. "There are two interesting fellows over there though." She pointed toward a table located on an elevated deck piece almost twenty feet away.

When Hali shifted, she realized the men at the table had been watching them. They averted their eyes quickly, but not quickly enough to cover their point of interest.

"They've been watching the tournament peeps too," Carrie said in a low voice. "The second you sat down, however, you became their point of interest."

"I wonder what that's about," Hali mused.

From his spot across from her, Gray made a growling sound that surprised Hali right down to her marrow.

"What is it?" she demanded as she studied his face. That wasn't his normal growl. It wasn't even his territorial "don't hit on my girlfriend" growl. No, this was something else entirely.

Gray slowly moved his eyes back to her. "They're shark shifters," he said in a low voice.

Hali waited for him to expand. When he didn't, she turned back to the men in question. They were getting to their feet. Not to leave though. No, they were heading in their direction.

"Uh-oh," Carrie muttered. "Is there going to be a fight? It looks like there's going to be a fight."

"There's not going to be a fight," Gray assured her, his eyes darting back to the shifters before sliding to Hali. "Baby, can you do me a favor and move right next to me over here?" He indicated the open chair to his right.

Hali didn't take time to consider why he was asking the question, or if she should turn him down. She knew he wouldn't have asked unless it was important. She immediately switched to the chair he'd indicated and watched as the shifters approached. She wasn't an expert on shifter politics, but recognized he wanted the upper hand when they introduced themselves. That's why he needed to remain in his seat.

"Hello," one of the men said in greeting as he glanced between faces. "May we join you?"

"Of course," Gray replied easily. To outside observers, he likely looked calm. Hali recognized he was on edge, however. "Please have a seat."

Carrie moved back so the shark shifters could take the open chairs. She looked perplexed, but she didn't question the meeting of minds. "You guys want more beers?" she asked the shifters.

"Yes, please," the first shifter who spoke replied. "Thank you."

Carrie cast Hali one more look and then headed toward the bar to collect the drinks. She looked worried, but there was nothing she could do to ease the tension at the table.

"I'm Ripley Harris," the shifter announced, extending his hand toward Gray. It was a sign of deference. "Everybody calls me Rip though. This is my associate, who also happens to be my brother, Finn."

Hali's mouth dropped open as Gray shook the shifter's hand. "Rip and Finn?"

Finn's eyebrows drew together. "Is that a problem?"

"Finn?" she repeated. "As in shark fin?"

Gray shot Hali a quelling look, but the wonder on her face stopped him. Hali was Hali, and he absolutely adored her. If she wanted to irritate the shifters, who was he to stop her?

"I guess I never thought about it," Rip mused. "It is kind of funny." He shot an amused look toward Hali. "What's your name?"

"Hali Waverly," she replied, not missing a beat.

"And you?" Rip glanced back at Gray.

"Grayson Hunter," he replied, not missing a beat. "You can call me Gray, though."

"Hmm." Rip's expression was hard to read. "You're not fully one of us, and yet you're strong in our ways."

Hali shifted on her chair. Gray had always been dubious when talking about his shark shifter heritage. This was the second time in as many days that somebody had commented about Gray's shark lines being strong. She had questions. She knew better than to seek answers just now.

"I'm more than one thing," Gray agreed as he squeezed Hali's hand. "You were in the water the other day. You saw us on the beach." It wasn't a question.

"That was me," Finn interjected, speaking for the first time. "I saw you. Given how you were looking at one another, I thought there was a chance I was going to be able to watch you go at each other on the beach. That didn't happen though."

Hali's lips curved down. "Is that your kink or something?"

Finn shrugged. "You're hot. What can I say?"

"Ignore him," Rip admonished when Gray's growl returned with a vengeance. "He's just messing with you. He doesn't actually watch people diddle each other on the beach." He paused a beat. "Wait. You don't really do that, do you?"

Finn merely shrugged in response.

Rip waved him off. "We're here for the tournament. We've

been getting the lay of the land. It seems this territory belongs to the two of you."

That was news to Hali. "I don't think I would phrase it that way."

"You didn't," Rip replied evenly. "It's the others in the area who described it that way. Every paranormal we've come into contact with says you two are the powers on the beach."

Carrie picked that moment to return with their drinks. She'd clearly heard the last part of the conversation because her eyes went wide as she slid Hali's Corona in front of her. "Everything okay here?" she asked pointedly as she delivered the other drinks.

Rip looked amused at the question. "I take it you're close with Hali," he assumed. "Are you as powerful as she is?"

"Not even close," Carrie replied, not missing a beat. "I'm the mashed potatoes on the side of the ribeye. She's the main course."

Hali balked. "That's not true."

"I'm fine with my lot in life," Carrie replied, her eyes on Rip. "Just for the record, though, if you try to cause problems here—if you hurt my friends—you'll see just how mean I can be. I might not be as powerful as Hali, but I'm way more diabolical." There was genuine warning in Carrie's tone.

Rip didn't seem worried about the threat. Instead, he burst out laughing. "I like your fiery personality."

"You won't if things go poorly." Carrie lowered her voice. "I don't know what the plan is here, but I'm hardly the only one watching you. Keep it civil."

"I notice you don't warn these two about keeping it civil," Finn said, gesturing toward Hali and Gray.

"Hali and I have been best friends since we were five," Carrie replied. "She has a free pass to do whatever she wants. I trust her. Gray gets a pass because she trusts him. I don't know you."

"I like how blunt you are," Finn noted. "Perhaps, when this conversation is over, we can say blunt things to one another?" He looked invested in the possibility.

"Oh, sorry," Carrie drawled. "You're not my type."

Finn's disappointment was obvious. "That's too bad."

"There are plenty more fish in the sea," Carrie replied. "Something tells me you'll be okay." She cast one more look toward Hali, a lifetime of friendship and trust coursing between them, and then took a step back. "I'll check on the trivia geeks and make my way around again. You guys play nice."

Once she was gone, the table devolved into silence for almost a full minute. Hali was the first to break it.

"Nobody wants any trouble here," she said. "How about we just lay out how we expect this to go and then part as happy acquaintances?"

Gray darted a look toward her, going soft all over at her earnest expression. "Nobody is going to throw down, baby," he assured her, gathering her hand and pressing it to his chest to calm her. "We're just feeling each other out."

"That's an apt assessment," Rip agreed. "How did you end up here?" he asked Gray. "Are you pack?"

"No." Gray shook his head. "I was raised in a wolf community but separated from them as an adult. I'm not associated with a pack but have friends who are still in the life."

"And your shark side? Do you embrace it?"

Gray hesitated and then held out his hands. "I haven't spent a lot of time with any of the local groups."

"Do you want to?"

"I don't know." Gray opted for honesty. "I need to think about it. I guess I wouldn't be opposed to it. My plate is pretty full right now though."

Rip's gaze slid to Hali. "So I see."

Hali narrowed her eyes in response. "Don't look at me that way," she warned.

"And what way am I looking at you?"

"As if you want to chomp me. Trust me. I'm way too big of a bite for you to chew."

Rip broke out into a wide grin. "I find you absolutely delightful. I prefer my women sleek and relentless, but if I was going to go for a witch, you would be on the top of my list."

Gray cleared his throat pointedly and drew Rip's gaze back to him. "Are you part of the tournament circuit?"

"In a manner of speaking," Rip replied, turning serious. "We're ... handling some of the action on the beach this week."

It took Hali a moment to grasp what he was getting at. "Wait, you're a loan shark who is an actual shark? That's a bit hokey, isn't it?"

Finn murdered Hali with one glare. "Why don't you speak a little louder? I don't think they heard you in the cheap seats down by the beach."

Hali didn't back down. "Nobody can hear anything—even with super special shifter hearing—when the music is playing," she shot back. "Also, even if some rando did hear me, they would have no idea what I was saying. There's no reason to get worked up."

"You could still be a little less jovial when discussing us," Finn insisted. "You look as if you're fighting the urge to laugh."

"That's because I am."

Gray moved his hand to Hali's knee under the table and gave her a pointed squeeze. Realizing she was taking over the conversation, Hali pressed her lips together to silence herself and allowed Gray control of the conversation once again.

"You're taking bets on the tournament," Gray deduced. "I didn't think about it before, but it makes sense."

"We don't follow the tournament or anything," Rip explained. "St. Pete is simply part of our region. We operate out of Treasure Island."

Hali's mouth dropped open again. "Treasure Island?" She couldn't help herself. "You guys are just embracing the stereotypes, aren't you?"

Rip didn't react by yelling. Instead, he arched an eyebrow. "Don't you own a bar called the Salty Cauldron? As a witch, isn't that a stereotype?"

"Yeah, I don't think I want to play this game any longer," Hali groused, folding her arms across her chest.

Gray chuckled. "Let's not fight about tedious stuff," he said. "Why is it you're here?"

"I just told you," Rip replied blankly.

"Not in St. Pete. Why are you at this bar tonight? Why did you decide to join us?"

"Oh." Rip held out his hands. "The bar looked fun. We could hear the music from the water. As for you two, we've been intrigued ever since we saw you on the beach the other night," he explained. "There was power rippling from both of you. We were curious if you were individually supplying that power, or if it was something more."

"Meaning what?" Gray asked, curious despite himself.

"Meaning that I've come to the conclusion that it is your bond that heightens your powers," he replied. "I don't know if you were lacking in shark shifter magic before—it might explain why you've never felt a kinship with the people on that side of the shoreline—but now your shark shifter genes are calling out to be utilized. Before it's all said and done, you will shift ... and you might find you're more shark than wolf."

Hali glanced at Gray's strong jaw. It was hard to ascertain how he felt about the revelation. "And you think the shark side of him is suddenly springing up because of me?" she asked after several seconds.

"I think you two have the sort of bond power-hungry people clamor for," Rip replied. "I've seen bonded mates before, but you two are something else entirely. Your magic feeds off the other person, whether you realize it or not."

Hali had no idea what to say to that. "Well, I guess that will keep the sex interesting," she said after what felt like a really long time.

Rip chuckled and drew a business card out of his pocket to hand to Gray. "Your life barrel is overflowing right now. When you have time—and the inclination—give me a call. I might be able to help you."

Gray studied the card for a moment and then tucked it into his wallet. "Thank you."

"As for the tournament, we expect to get in and out fast," Rip said. "You have nothing to worry about."

"That would be a nice change of pace for us," Gray acknowledged.

After twenty more minutes of conversation, the shark shifters departed, and Hali and Gray were left to sift through the conversation.

"That was weird, right?" Hali demanded.

"It was, and I'm not entirely certain they're telling the truth about their motivations," Gray admitted. "I have no reason to doubt them, and yet I do."

"What do you want to do?"

"I want to start herding Dominic back toward the resort. He can bring the blonde if he wants. I don't want to be out here all night though."

Hali nodded in understanding. "I think that can be arranged. I'll threaten his manhood if he doesn't comply."

Gray broke out in a wide smile. "I really do adore you, Hali Waverly."

"Even though I say stupid things in front of dangerous shifters?"

"Even though," he confirmed. "I happen to love everything that comes out of your mouth."

"I'm going to remind you of that statement next time you're annoyed with me."

"I'm looking forward to it."

ELEVEN

D ominic whined the whole way back to the resort. Hali kept her attention on him, leaving Gray to constantly scan the beach behind them for signs of movement or an incoming enemy.

"You ruined my night," the trivia guru groused when they dropped him off at his door. "I was about to get lucky."

"She was too young for you," Gray shot back. "Start fishing in age-appropriate waters, and I'll leave you alone."

Dominic scowled. "You know, I find it rich that you're screwing with my love life when you have this queen at your side." He beamed at Hali. "He's mean. He's got his and wants to keep others from getting what they deserve. Perhaps you would like to trade up."

Hali blinked several times and then pasted a fake smile on her face. "I think I'm good."

"Of course you are." Dominic made an exasperated sound in the base of his throat. "This sucks. Next time I go to an event, I'm going to make sure that nobody there is more attractive than me. I'm not going through this again."

That struck Hali as legitimately funny, and she let loose a giggle. "Somehow I think you're going to survive."

"Whatever."

Once they were reasonably assured Dominic was locked away for the night and not liable to leave—there was no controlling him should he decide he needed to pick someone up, so they refused to focus on it—the couple headed to the villa. Hali slipped her hand in his for the walk, Gray picking a deliberately slow pace.

"I'm okay," she said to him in a low voice when she noticed exactly how slow their progress was. "You don't have to worry about me."

Gray lifted one shoulder in a haphazard shrug. "I happen to think it's a beautiful night. Why not enjoy it?"

"We could be enjoying it more in bed."

"We have time." He kept a firm hold on her hand and scanned the beach before taking the turn on the side walkway that led to her home. "How is your hip?"

She bit back a sigh, but just barely. "I don't like talking about my hip."

"I know, but I happen to like you, and your hip is attached to you."

"You just like swooping in and being a hero."

"That too." He refused to get into an argument with her. He also refused to pretend there wasn't an issue. "I care about you, Hali. I don't like seeing you in pain. It's not in my nature to ignore that pain. That means we're going to be talking about the hip going forward."

Hali's scowl was pronounced. "I don't like looking weak."

"I know. For the record, you couldn't look weak even if you tried. You're one of the strongest people I know. Your hip does not make you weak." He was calm when he leveled his gaze on her. "I hate thinking you're in pain. I can't help it."

She sighed and shook her head. "It's just worse at night. I barely feel it when I wake up."

He knew that wasn't true. He also knew she wasn't at a place where she was ready to talk about it. He had to let it go, or they would constantly argue, and that wasn't what he wanted. "Give me your opinion on what went down tonight. What do you think of Rip and Finn?"

"Blowhards," she replied, not missing a beat. "They're full of themselves. I think the gambling angle is interesting, but that doesn't mean they had anything to do with what happened to Brian Parker."

"I happen to agree. I'm interested in why you think that though."

"Well, for starters, you don't kill the person who owes you money. You just maim them. Everybody knows that."

"I do love a good maiming," Gray said on a laugh.

"I can't see why they would care about the questions either," Hali continued. "It's the people answering the questions who are important to what they're doing. Changing the questions—unless they somehow have knowledge of one of the contestants having access to those questions—doesn't make a lot of sense to me."

"I don't disagree." Gray took Hali's keycard from her when they arrived at her door and waved it in front of her scanner. When it opened, he shoved his foot in the opening and swung her into his arms, earning a sputter and a giggle for his efforts.

"What are you doing?" she demanded.

"Sweeping you off your feet."

"I told you that I'm fine walking on my own. I'm not in pain."

"You are in pain. I still let you walk on your own. My goal now is to romance you until you pass out from exhaustion. This is merely the first step in that process."

Hali puffed out a sigh. "Fine, but this hip thing is going to turn into a bone of contention between us at some point. I need to do this on my own timetable."

Her earnest expression tugged at Gray's heartstrings. "I know. I'll try not to push too much. There will be times I get frustrated, though."

"I know." Her fingertips were light as she brushed them over his cheek. "We're both too alpha for our own good. That means we're going to fight."

"Then we'll fight. Just as long as we make up, I'm good."

Hali laughed. "Why am I not surprised about that?"

"Because you know me well."

"I feel as if I really am getting to know you well."

He leaned in and gave her a soft kiss. "Me, too. It's going to be okay. I can't just ignore it when you're in pain, but I don't want to change you. I don't want to control you. I just want to be there for you."

"You've been there for me since you crashed into my life."

"I feel the same way about you. We'll figure it out."

"Can we start figuring it out tomorrow? I want to focus on you for the rest of the night. No distractions."

"That right there is the best offer I've had all day."

MORNINGS WERE HALI'S FAVORITE PART OF the day. The resort was quiet before nine o'clock. Even the beach walkers didn't speak to one another. They simply walked up and down the sand, occasionally bobbing their heads at one another, and seemingly marveling at the softly rolling waves. Hali enjoyed a good beach walk. She liked beach yoga a little less. Drinking coffee on her back patio was one of her favorite pastimes, however, even though the space belonged to Wayne now.

"Ugh." Hali wrinkled her nose when she got a whiff of the

bird, who was on the cement between the fence and one of the chairs. "Why do you smell like a brewery?"

Wayne was still awake, but his unfocused gaze told Hali all she needed to know about his mental status. He would be passing out quickly. "I happen to think I smell divine," he drawled.

"Of course you do." Hali looked up when a shirtless Gray slipped through the back door. "Maybe we should go back inside. He smells ... not good."

Gray frowned when he caught sight of the flamingo. "I thought I was doing you a favor when I relegated him to this space, but apparently that's not the case. Is there another place we can set up for him as a nest? Or is it a burrow? Like ... where do the other flamingos hang out?"

For some reason, the question struck Hali as funny. "Have you not noticed the lack of flamingos in this area? That's why he stands out. There are a few here or there, but most of them are migrating when you see them. This is not their natural habitat. Why do you think Wayne spends all his time hitting on the egrets?"

"I thought he just assumed they were pale flamingos. What? The bird is blind drunk constantly. I don't know his natural habitat."

Hali laughed again and then shook her head. "Most people assume he's a pet released in the wild. He's become a conversation piece here for a reason."

"That reason is that I'm an absolute delight," Wayne replied. He was barely awake. "You can't move me elsewhere anyway. I'm Hali's flamingo. I'm her protector. That means I have to be close."

"Yes, you're doing a fabulous job protecting her," Gray deadpanned. "I mean ... the merrow seem terrified of you."

"Whatever. I'm on top of things." Wayne waved a wing. "I'm so good at my job, I watched the man in black work on the trivia stage for two straight hours before dawn ... and it had nothing to do with the edibles that couple from Indiana left behind in one of the cabanas."

"What man in black?" Hali asked as she sipped her coffee.

"I don't know." Wayne didn't look all that interested in the topic, even though he was the one who had brought it up. "There was a guy out there. He was installing things under the stage. I think it was speakers or something."

Hali frowned. "No. The speakers were installed yesterday morning. We saw them doing it."

"Plus, they used the already installed speakers during the preliminary rounds yesterday," Gray added. "The sound system was fine."

"Why would they be installing speakers before dawn anyway?"

"I don't know." Gray's forehead filled with troubled lines. "Are you sure it was speakers that were being installed?"

"How should I know?" Wayne barked. "They put three boxes under the stage. They seemed intent. I just assumed they were speakers."

On a grimace, Gray drained the rest of his coffee and focused on Hali. "I don't like it," he said finally. "That doesn't sound normal to me."

"You want to check out the stage before anybody is out there this morning," she surmised.

"Are you okay with that?"

There was no hesitation on her part. "I am. I think we should head out there first thing. We'll worry about breakfast after."

"Yeah, I think we'll both be more comfortable with that."

GRAY'S EYES WERE KEEN AS THEY SCANNED THE BEACH upon their arrival at the trivia stage. Security was nonexistent for the space. They'd put up ropes to block it off, but there were no guards to keep people away, and the ropes wouldn't stop anybody who really wanted to cross.

"You stay here and watch for interlopers," Gray instructed as he moved off the sidewalk, leaving Hali to glare in his wake. "I'll be right back."

"Are you kidding me?" Hali refused to be left behind and stalked into the sand after him. "I'm not staying over there where it's safe while you put your life on the line."

"How do you know I'm putting my life on the line?" Gray demanded as he dropped to his knees next to the stage. "It really could be speakers."

Hali gave him a "whatever" look.

"Fine. Just get ready to run if I issue an order."

"Yeah, I'm going to do what I want." Hali was careful when dropping down next to him. She leaned in when Gray lifted the skirt so they could see underneath the stage. It was dark enough that both of them had to wait for their eyes to adjust. Then, sure enough, a box came into view on their right.

"I can't see what that is," Gray complained.

"Hold up." Hali glanced over her shoulder to scan the beach. Finding it empty, she waved her hand and watched as her fingers ignited with magical fire. A soothing green light illuminated the space beneath the stage and allowed Gray to get a closer look at what they were dealing with. It didn't take him long before he blanched.

"Oh, crap." He grabbed Hali around the waist and dragged her away from the stage, ignoring the way she sputtered and waved her hands to snuff out the flames.

"What's wrong?" Hali barked as she rolled to her back and stared up into his face.

Gray was on all fours above her, giving him the dominant position. There was nothing flirty about the way he looked down at his girlfriend, however. In fact, he appeared to be considering panicking. "Baby, that's a bomb."

Hali's mouth ran dry. "Are you kidding me?"

"No, I am not. There's a countdown clock. I saw it. I can smell the C-4 too."

Hali took a moment to absorb the information. "What time is it supposed to go off?"

"Three hours from now."

She did the math in her head. "That's about an hour after the first round starts."

"I think it's fair to say that the contestants are the target," Gray acknowledged. "When we were leaving, Wayne told us he saw three boxes total. I'm guessing that means three bombs because there's no controlling where people sit. Whoever set those things will want to cover every angle."

It made sense to Hali. "So, what do we do?"

"I don't know." Gray blinked twice. "My first instinct is to call the police. I'm not sure that's the right instinct though."

"Why?" Hali was honestly curious.

"Because, if we can defuse those bombs and remove them without anybody noticing, we might be able to gauge who set them just by monitoring the crowd. If there's a specific face who isn't there..." He trailed off.

"Oh, right." Hali moved her eyes back to the stage. "Do you know how to defuse them?"

"In theory. I'm not keen on doing it with you by my side though in case I make a mistake. I'll be a nervous wreck worrying something is going to happen to you."

"And being nervous means you'll be more prone to making mistakes," Hali surmised. "What if we did it together?"

"What do you mean?" Gray's eyes lit with intrigue.

"I'll use my magic to protect us while you defuse them.

We'll move between units, and then remove them when we're done."

Gray didn't look convinced. "How do you know you can protect us?"

"Because I'm nowhere near done with you." Hali managed a smile. "I trust us a heckuva lot more than I trust outsiders. We can do this."

Gray leaned down and stared directly into her eyes. "I don't want to put you at risk."

"Others will be at risk if we don't do this."

Gray nodded and sighed. "Fine. I'm the boss though."

"That sounds kinky."

"Oh, I'm going to need a few hours before we play *that* game," he complained. "Let's do it, though. You're right. I trust you and me a lot more than I do anybody else."

"I'm right there with you."

IT WAS A TENSE AFFAIR. MORE THAN ONCE, Gray was convinced he was going to flub something and blow them both to smithereens. Hali was eternally calm as she encased them in a magical shield, however, and they methodically moved through the bombs. Once defused, Gray removed any dangerous wires and separated the C-4 from the blasting agents. They were on the last bomb, and both of them were starting to feel anxious.

"Make sure nobody is coming, Hali," Gray ordered. "I've almost got this."

Her hand pressed to his chest, the steady beat of his heart holding the protection shield in place, Hali did as he instructed. "There are people down on the beach," she said as he killed the timer and started pulling wires. "They're nowhere near us though."

"Okay." Gray chewed on his bottom lip as he removed the

wires and then separated the blasting cap from the actual explosive, handing the now useless C-4 to her and keeping the item that could still explode near him. "That's it."

"Are we sure?" Hali asked. She wanted to be done. Still, part of her was worried. "I don't consider Wayne the best source of information. Just because he said there were only three bombs, that doesn't necessarily mean he was right."

"Good point." Gray placed a smacking kiss against her forehead before rolling to his knees. He prowled the entire length of the stage, backward and forward, and then rolled back on his haunches several feet away from her. "I can't see anything else."

"Here." Hali handed him the C-4 and rolled under the stage, using her magic to illuminate the area before she scanned it. She kept her eyes closed for several seconds, and then blew out a breath when she was finished. "I can't find anything else either."

"That's good, right?"

She shrugged, giggling when he grabbed her ankle and pulled her out from underneath the stage. "What are you doing?"

"This." Gray tugged her in for a tight hug, briefly burying his face in her hair. "That freaked me out," he admitted.

"I've never dealt with explosives before." Hali was comfortable in his arms, so she didn't make a move to leave the warmth of his embrace. "I'm used to magical enemies. It feels somehow different."

"Yeah." Gray rubbed his hands up and down her back. "This was unexpected."

"And to think, people might've died if it wasn't for Wayne."

Her tone struck Gray as funny. "Maybe we should try to sober him up."

Hali looked horrified at the thought. "Or we could just let him hit rock bottom and handle his own problems."

"I'm going to leave that decision to you," Gray replied, his gaze going to the explosives. "We need to get this stuff out of here, and we need to do it in a way that doesn't draw attention."

"I could call for two room service carts," Hali replied. "They're covered underneath with tablecloths. Cecily could arrange it. We need to keep the firing mechanism and the C-4 separate, right?"

"Yeah. Then we need to get both out of here." Gray looked momentarily lost in thought. "Rusty knows a thing or two about explosives. He might be able to help us."

"I don't even want to know why he's an expert on explosives," Hali groused.

"Construction. He's been part of a few building demolitions. It's part of the game."

"Oh." Hali looked momentarily thoughtful. "If you think he could help, then let's go for it. Franklin isn't going to want a big deal made out of this, so he'll do whatever is necessary to get the explosives off the grounds without anybody noticing."

"Yeah." Gray was grim when he nodded. "That's exactly what I'm counting on."

TWELVE

Rusty met Gray and Hali at the villa. It was the easiest place to hand over the bombs. He was curious as he studied the materials that had been separated, shaking his head when he held up the C-4.

"It wouldn't have been a big explosion," he said. "I only briefly saw the stage, but I'm not sure it would've taken the whole thing out."

"There were three bombs, evenly dispersed," Gray pointed out.

"Okay, so maybe it would've taken the whole stage out. It wouldn't have done a lot of damage to the surrounding area."

"So, it had to be targeted." Gray stretched his arms over his head. Now that the bombs were being removed from the premises, some of the tension he'd been feeling had begun to dissipate. "Why target trivia contestants?"

"I think that's your question to answer." Rusty took one of the boxes and moved it into the back of his truck. "I can try to figure out where the C-4 came from. There aren't a lot of guys dealing in it around these parts. I don't know what help I can offer you other than to get rid of it, though."

"Are we certain we shouldn't give it to the cops?" Hali queried. "Shouldn't they be made aware of this?"

Gray lifted one shoulder in a shrug. "I think it's too late now. We both agreed in the moment that we wanted to be the ones to defuse the bombs. We're going to get in trouble if we call them now."

"Even Andrew?"

Gray could read the unease rolling off her. He wanted to soothe her, but he had very little to offer in the moment. "Even Andrew," he confirmed.

Hali exhaled heavily on a nod. "Okay. This is more your area of expertise than mine."

"It's a long shot to find who bought the C-4," Rusty said. "We might luck out though."

"I just want it off the grounds at this point," Gray supplied. "The plan is to be watching the stage at the time the bombs were scheduled to go off. We might see someone slinking away, or someone acting frustrated because the plan didn't play out."

"Then what?" Rusty queried. "What are you going to do without proof if you find this individual?"

"I have no idea." Gray was rueful. "Right now, we're playing Russian Roulette in the dark. I just don't know."

"Well, keep your witch safe, huh?" Rusty slung an arm around Hali's shoulders and dropped a kiss on top of her head. "I happen to like her."

"You just like my best friend," Hali countered.

"I'm not convinced that she won't fall in love with me yet," Rusty argued. "I know she says I'm not her type, but what if she's wrong?"

"Oh, whatever." Hali huffed out a breath. "You know she's not going to fall for you whatever you do. You just like attention."

"See, you know me." Rusty winked, gave her another

squeeze, and then released her. "I'm seriously brokenhearted over the Carrie situation though. I think that means you're going to have to find a suitable woman for me to hook up with in the foreseeable future to ease my broken heart."

Gray rolled his eyes so hard it was a miracle he didn't fall over. "Like you have trouble finding women."

"I want the right woman," Rusty countered. "You're happy with your witch. Why can't I be happy too?"

Gray studied his brother for a long beat and then held out his hands. "If I thought you were being serious, I might actually try to help. I happen to believe you're just blowing smoke, however."

"That's a hurtful thing to say about your brother."

"It's the truth, though, isn't it?"

"Maybe." Rusty winked and then grabbed the other box of supplies. "I'll be in touch." He hesitated, as if he was debating saying something, and then continued. "Mom and Dad asked about you this morning."

Gray froze. "Oh, yeah?" His voice was deceptively calm. "And what were they asking about? I'm guessing it wasn't flattering, whatever the conversation stemmed from."

"They heard you were dating a witch." Rusty shot Hali an apologetic look. "They're not happy."

"I don't really care what they think." Gray was firm. "I happen to like my witch."

"I know you do. I said I liked her too. They're just ... being themselves."

"Good for them. I guess."

"I just don't want you to be surprised if they show up out of the blue and suddenly show an interest in your life," Rusty said in a low voice. "They might've been mortified by you standing up to the chief, but that doesn't mean they didn't have plans for bringing you back into the fold at some point. I don't want you showing your back to them. You know how they are."

Hali glanced between brothers, her anxiety ratcheting up a notch. Her family was stressful, but not in the same way as what Gray was used to. "Maybe I should meet them," she volunteered out of the blue. "They might like me even if they don't want to."

Gray rested his hand on her shoulder. "I don't think that's a smart choice, baby. I don't want to seek them out for my own reasons. No matter what, though, they won't like you because you're not pack."

"They're jerks," Rusty confirmed. "I want to smack them around on a regular basis. You shouldn't worry about them. You're way better than they could ever dream of being."

Hali didn't look convinced. "Well, I guess we'll have to wait and see if they stop in for a visit."

"I don't think it's happening today or anything," Rusty assured them. "It's more that I feel them laying the ground-work. If they do show up, I don't think it will be for a few weeks. I just want you to be prepared."

"Thanks." Gray offered his brother a one-armed bro-dude hug because that was their way. "I appreciate the heads-up. They're really not part of my life any longer, though. I don't care what they think."

"No, you just care about Hali." Rusty offered up a playful wink to the witch in question. "I get it. I don't blame you for wanting to keep them at a distance. I just wanted to warn you. You can't keep Mom and Dad out of your business forever."

A muscle worked in Gray's jaw, but he forced a smile. "You're the only Hunter I want in my life right now. Thanks for the heads-up though."

"Don't mention it."

. . .

HALI HAD QUESTIONS. GRAY RARELY TALKED
about his parents. She was aware of the situation that got him
booted from the pack. One of the pack elders had tried to
take a teenage bride against her will, and Gray had intervened.
That made him a hero in her book. The pack thought differ-
ently. His own parents had shunned him in the aftermath.
That meant she would never like them. The question was, did
Gray want to keep them out of his life or was he just
covering?

"I can hear the gears of your mind working from here,"
Gray noted as they made their way from the villa toward the
tiki bar. The plan was for Hali to open the bar as usual, and
Gray to plant himself on a stool to watch the tournament.
There wasn't much else they could do. "If you have a ques-
tion, you might as well ask it."

"I have a lot of questions," Hali admitted as she
rummaged in her pocket for the tiki bar keys. "I'm afraid to
ask them though."

Gray jerked his eyes in her direction. The beach was
starting to fill up with people—the trivia crew was working
near the stage—but she was his sole focus. "Don't ever be
afraid to ask me questions. This isn't going to work if either of
us is afraid to tell the other exactly what they're feeling." He
moved his hands to her shoulders. "I really want this to work,
in case I haven't made that obvious."

Hali huffed out a breath and nodded. "Okay. Sit down
over there." She pointed toward his usual stool. "I'll get you an
iced tea and ask my questions."

"Okay." Gray did as instructed. He knew her morning
routine for opening the bar almost as well as she did at this
point. Several seconds after she rolled up the tiki window, she
handed him the iced tea. She'd turned on the blenders and had
the cash drawer out so she could dole out the change before he
even started cataloging her movements.

"Do you want your parents in your life again?" she asked straightaway.

"Wow, and here I thought you were going to ease into things," he teased before sucking on his straw. "As for my parents, no, I don't want them in my life."

"Are you sure?"

Gray nodded. "Hali, they're not like your parents."

"There have been times when I've considered shutting my parents out of my life," Hali said solemnly. "I get it."

"That's a load of crap." Gray said it in an affable way despite the harshness of the words. "I can see you getting angry at your parents when you were younger, doing the typical teenager thing. You never once considered shutting them out of your life, however. Don't be ridiculous."

Hali was sheepish. "Fine. I think that's my problem though. No matter how angry I got at my parents—and there were times I wanted to throttle them when growing up—I always knew they would be there for me in a pinch. Your parents aren't that way."

"No, they most certainly are not."

"I want to hurt them because they hurt you."

"That's sweet."

She made a face. "I also want to be there for you, but I don't know how. If you want your parents in your life, I can help. I don't have to be around when you meet with them. I can make myself scarce."

The suggestion rankled Gray to his very marrow. "Hali, that's not okay with me. In an ideal world, would I prefer my parents admit they'd been wrong about everything, ask my forgiveness, and fall in love with you? Absolutely. That's not going to happen though."

He grabbed her hands and held tightly. "I know we haven't been dating for very long, and this might come out sounding a bit heavy, but I see my future when I look at you. I don't say that to scare you," he added quickly. "I just don't want a life without you. That means I will not allow you to be verbally abused by them. I can't stand by and let that happen. I won't."

"Maybe they won't hate me," Hali suggested. "Maybe they're growing as people."

"Oh, you're so cute." Gray leaned in and pressed a heart-felt kiss to her forehead. "My parents are not the sort to grow. They'll expect me to be the one who compromises everything, including my morals, to return to the fold. I'm not doing that, Hali."

"I just can't imagine being completely on your own for so long."

"I had Rusty. Now I have you."

"You definitely have me." She blew out a sigh. "You can have my parents and siblings if you want too."

It took everything Gray had to keep a straight face. "That's a lovely offer. I don't want to steal them from you though."

"It's not theft if it's freely given."

"Yeah, now you're just trying to torture me."

Hali broke out into a wide grin. "I like to keep things fresh."

"You're good at it."

THE TIKI BAR WAS BUSY DURING THE trivia rounds, but most of the guests took their drinks and moved closer to the stage rather than hang out on the patio. The time the bombs were scheduled to go off came and went, and no matter how hard he scanned the sidewalk and beach, Gray found nothing out of the ordinary. Whoever had set the bombs obviously hadn't hung out to watch the aftermath.

"Maybe whoever did it realized we removed the bombs so there was no reason to act surprised when they didn't go off,"

Hali suggested as she stood next to Gray in the shade of a palm tree.

"It's possible," he confirmed.

"But you don't believe it."

"I don't know what I believe right now." He opted for honesty. "I think it could go either way. I—" Whatever he was going to say died on his lips when a shrill shriek emanated from the stage, drawing their attention in that direction.

"You can't be serious!" Vinessa "Vinnie" Dawson hopped to her feet and shook her fist. "There's no way that I fell behind the rest of these reprobates. I'm way smarter than them."

Confused, Hali's eyebrows moved toward one another. "What happened?"

"I'm not sure." Gray slid his arm around her waist, anchoring her to his side. He was still marveling at the way she'd tried to sacrifice herself to give him what she thought he needed to repair things with his parents hours before. It wasn't what he needed, but she was willing to give regardless. To him, that made her magical.

"She was ousted," Annabelle volunteered. Instead of sitting at the bar, she'd opted to do her work at a small bistro table this afternoon, keeping one eye on the trivia contest while also answering emails and typing out briefs. "The round was close, but two of the contestants had to be eliminated. She was one of them."

Hali pursed her lips as she watched the woman—she was tall, something Hali didn't realize until she witnessed her towering over the other contestants—throw an absolute fit.

"Cheaters! You're all cheaters!" Vinnie insisted as she stomped her foot. "I can't believe you're all just sitting there and pretending that you're not cheating. I'm way smarter than you."

"She seems ... interesting," Gray mused, shaking his head.

"If you listen to the other contestants, she's not all that interesting," Annabelle countered. Her gaze was on her computer screen, but she was clearly listening to the melee. "Supposedly, she's married but hits on every other contestant within hearing distance ... as long as they too are married. Apparently, she doesn't care if they're male or female."

"I love an equal opportunity flirt," Hali drawled.

"She doesn't flirt with the single ones," Annabelle volunteered. "She only flirts with the married ones, or the taken ones." She finally lifted her eyes. "I saw her scoping out Gray when she was taking a bathroom break about an hour ago."

Hali was taken aback. "She was checking him out?"

"She was. She stood behind him for a good ten minutes, staring and trying to get his attention. Unfortunately for her, he was completely focused on you. He didn't even look up when she rubbed her boobs against his back under the pretense of grabbing a napkin."

"I don't even remember that happening," Gray admitted. "Are you sure that was actually a thing?"

"I'm very sure," Annabelle confirmed.

"Huh." Gray flicked his eyes to Hali. "Don't worry, baby, I only want you to press your boobs against my back."

Hali laughed. If there was one thing she wasn't worried about, it was Gray's fidelity. He wasn't a cheater. They had that in common. "I don't remember it happening either."

"I've been watching her," Annabelle explained. "She's ... interesting, but not in a good way."

"Then how is she interesting?" Hali queried.

"She's a game player. She doesn't flirt because she needs the attention. I wondered at first, but that's not who she is. Some people are like that. She might claim to be like that if ever called on her actions. She's being manipulative, though. She hits on the married men to make them uncomfortable.

She tells the married women that their men are probably being hit on too. It's all a mental game."

"She was eliminated, though," Gray noted. "Her games won't matter now."

"There's that," Annabelle agreed. "One of the guys she was flirting with was eliminated too." She pointed. "That's Chris Patterson. I looked him up. He does quite well on the circuit. He did poorly this time though."

"Because he was distracted by Vinnie?" Hali queried.

Annabelle held out her hands. "That's my guess. I can't be sure though. I just know that Vinnie wasn't expecting to be eliminated. She's not going to be happy, and she's not going to go away quietly."

Hali and Gray stood to the side, their shoulders touching, and watched as Vinnie walked around screaming about injustice and cheating. She was irate to the point of no return.

The other eliminated contestant was much quieter, although he didn't look any happier about what had transpired.

"What do you think?" Gray asked in a low voice after several minutes of watching the drama play out.

"I think that Vinnie is a poor loser."

"Yeah, I'll be interested to see if she hangs around for the rest of the tournament or heads home."

"You think she'll stay?" The possibility hadn't even occurred to Hali.

"I think it depends on what her goals are here. It's possible she doesn't even really care about winning. I mean, the money would be nice, but I think maybe she likes the psychological game more."

"Do you think that somehow ties into our bombs?"

"I don't see how, but I'm not willing to rule anything out." Gray moved his hand to Hali's back and began to lightly rub at the tension she was carrying between her shoulders.

"What do you think about the other guy?" He inclined his head toward Chris. "He's clearly mad but not showing it the same way Vinnie is."

"I think he's much more likely to be a lone bomber," Hali replied, not missing a beat. "Would he set bombs knowing he was going to be sitting on the stage though?"

"Good point." Gray shifted his gaze off the stage and around the beach. A lot of people were watching the show. He recognized a few faces, but not most of them. "I would have to think that whoever set that bomb isn't a participant."

"So, it's someone with an outside interest," Hali mused. "The thing is, not all the contestants were on the stage this morning. They had two preliminary rounds before moving to the quarterfinals." She pointed toward the current roster of talent. "Maybe someone was aiming for someone in that first round of contestants."

"Now that there is an idea." Gray stroked his chin. "I think I'll ask Cecily if she can get me a list of who was on the stage and when."

"It can't possibly hurt, right?"

"That's exactly what I was thinking."

THIRTEEN

Dominic appeared more than eager to follow a blonde away from the resort when things were wrapping up for the day. Gray caught him by the back of the shirt before he could scamper off.

"Don't even think about it," he warned.

Dominic scowled in protest. "You're ruining my vibe."

"You'll live." Gray dragged him toward the tiki bar and deposited him at one of the patio tables. "If you want to pick up someone, you can do it from here."

"There's only one hot woman here," Dominic complained. "I'm pretty sure she's spoken for too." He gestured toward Hali.

"Hey!" Annabelle, who had moved to one of the stools next to the bar, jerked up her head. "What did you just say?"

Dominic balked. "I didn't see you there," he replied automatically.

"Right." Annabelle made a face. "Whatever."

"It's true," Dominic whined. "If I'd seen you sitting there, I totally would've hit on you. You have that stern thing I love so much. I bet you're bossy when the lights go off and the nudity comes out."

"How lovely," she drawled.

Hali smirked as she rested her palms on the counter. "What do you want?" she asked Dominic.

"Sex," he replied. "Are you offering?"

Gray slapped his hand against Dominic's shoulder a little harder than was necessary. "Are you seriously going to push me when things have been going so well between us?"

"Who said I was pushing you?"

"I would think that's a given."

Dominic blew out a sigh. "Give me one of those blue things."

"One Mermaid's Tail coming right up," Hali confirmed as she started gathering ingredients.

Even though Gray wanted to sit closer to her, he figured it was wise to keep an eye on Dominic. The guy was slippery, and Gray could see him slinking away if he got distracted. On top of that, Dominic was in on all the gossip from the tournament. Now was as good a time as any to collect that gossip.

"Tell me about the woman who melted down at the end there," Gray ordered as he got comfortable across from Dominic. He was all smiles when Hali delivered the cocktail and a glass of iced tea for him. "Thank you." He lightly patted her hip. "You're my favorite bartender ever."

Hali smirked. "You're only saying that because you don't want to sleep on the couch tonight."

The couch was way too small for Gray's bulky frame. He didn't mention that though. "I'm saying it because it's true," he countered. "Nobody in the history of the world has ever bartended me better. Wait ... is that a word?"

"I'm not sure."

"It's a word," Dominic confirmed. "Probably not how you

meant it, but it's definitely a word." He sipped his drink and grinned. "I have to agree. You are the world's best bartender."

"Oh, thank you for the compliment," Hali replied. "Don't forget the gossip though. I want to hear your opinion on Vinnie."

"I've already told you my feelings on her," Dominic replied as he kicked back in his chair. "She's all surface, no substance."

"There has to be something inside of her," Hali argued. "Even if she puts on an external facade, there's something inside of her that's real." She slid her arm around Gray's shoulders and leaned into him.

Sensing that she might be trying to rest her hip without acknowledging she was resting her hip, Gray tugged her down on his lap.

"I'm working," she protested.

"You're resting for the next ten minutes," he countered. "Don't argue with me. The bar isn't busy. Kendra can handle any drink orders."

Hali glared at him but didn't move to stand up. That told Gray that he'd been right, and it was the exact right time to force a break on her.

"You want to hear the gossip anyway," Gray reminded her. "You might as well be comfortable for it."

"Who says I'm comfortable on your lap?" she challenged.

Rather than respond, Gray tickled her.

"Fine." She squirmed, fighting off a laugh. "I'm comfortable. Stop doing that!"

"Oh, you guys are so wholesome it makes me want to puke," Dominic complained, shaking his head. "Seriously, you could be a movie on the Hallmark Channel."

"Talk," Gray ordered. "We want to hear about the two people who were eliminated today."

"It was just the third round," Dominic replied, turning

serious. "I don't think she was paying attention. None of us normally pay attention this early. We just answer our questions and weed out the weak links."

"Does that mean there are no weak links in the current crop of contestants?" Gray queried, his fingers lightly massaging Hali's hip. She'd turned into a pile of butter on his lap, and he knew the hip was bothering her, whether she acknowledged it or not.

"Not really," Dominic replied. "Usually, the locals are knocked out early at these things, but you have three strong contenders from this area."

"Including Lana," Hali surmised, opening her eyes.

"She's good," Dominic acknowledged. "On top of that, she can't be easily distracted. I think there might be something wrong with her. You know, mentally."

"There's nothing wrong with her," Hali shot back. "She's just ... very focused."

"If you say so. I've tried flirting with her, though, and she's not interested. To me, that indicates there's something wrong with her."

"Or she's the smartest woman in the world," Gray countered as he continued to work on Hali's hip. "Tell me about this Vinnie woman," he instructed. "She seemed genuinely upset this afternoon. She can't be used to winning constantly. Why melt down over an early exit? I'm sure it's happened more than once."

"The purse on this one is huge," Dominic explained. "Like ... huge. Normally, we top out at a hundred grand. There's no money to be found if you bow out before the semi-finals either. She basically didn't even leave the show with a parting gift."

Realization dawned on Gray. "So, all the money she spent on the plane ticket and the hotel came out of her pocket."

Dominic nodded in affirmation. "Yup. That's how it

works. Normally, the upper echelon at least breaks even. She's mad because she won't break even."

"And what about that Chris guy?" Gray asked. "He seemed upset too."

"I don't know him as well." Dominic wrinkled his nose. "He's not new, but he doesn't travel to every tournament. He keeps east of the Mississippi River. He's a strong competitor and doesn't normally go out this early. He's not a complainer though."

"Someone said that he was flirting with Vinnie," Hali noted. "Could that have thrown him off?"

"Maybe, but she's tried with him before, and I've never seen it have an effect on him." Dominic shrugged. "That guy is an enigma."

That meant he had secrets, Gray mused. *How deep did those secrets run?*

GRAY CUT DOMINIC OFF AFTER THREE DRINKS and then directed him back toward the hotel.

"I'll be back to help you close when I've dropped him off in his room," Gray promised Hali, who was busy wiping down tables. "If someone shows up, lock yourself in the tiki hut. I won't be long."

Hali scowled at him. "I can take care of myself."

"I didn't say you couldn't. I just want to keep my girl safe."

Hali rolled her eyes in exaggerated fashion. "I've got it. Take a chill pill."

"You'd better watch your back." Gray wagged his finger. "I'll be back before you know it."

"I can't wait." Hali sang to herself as she cleaned. She didn't think she had much of a voice, although Gray had teasingly said she sang like a siren when he'd heard her in the shower one morning. She figured lust was blinding him, but she didn't mind risking potential embarrassment when she was alone. She was so lost in what she was singing, she almost missed a furtive movement at the corner of the patio. Thankfully, her inner danger alarm kicked in at the exact right moment, and she smoothly rounded to find the shark shifters watching her from the shadows.

The first emotion that registered upon recognizing Rip and Finn was relief. She'd assumed it was the merrow returning to either chat or throw down. After taking a breath, however, she was understandably suspicious.

"You guys are out late," she noted as she dumped some empty cups in the trash. She'd sent home Kendra an hour before and was glad for it. She didn't want to expose the woman to potential danger. "I'm sorry, but we're closing for the night. If you want a drink, you'll have to head down to the beach bar."

"It's awfully early to be closing, isn't it?" Rip queried as he glanced around. "It's only ten o'clock."

"It's midweek," Hali replied. "Also, the trivia contestants are dedicated and not rampant partiers. They're not staying out late."

"That can't be good for business."

"It's fine. I like an early week now and then."

"So you can spend time with your boyfriend?" Rip plopped down at one of the tables Hali had just cleaned. "You guys are an interesting duo."

Hali wasn't certain what to make of the observation. "Thanks. I guess."

Rip smirked. "It wasn't meant as an insult."

"I didn't take it as one."

"That's not what your demeanor change suggests. You're agitated."

Hali *was* agitated. She didn't like Rip or his presence at her bar. She was interested in shark shifters, at least on a superficial level. She wanted insight into Gray's strange upbringing. That didn't mean she trusted these two.

"What can I do for you?" she asked pointedly. "I'm sure you're not here to engage in harmless conversation. You have an agenda. It's best to just tell me what you want."

"What makes you think we want anything?" Finn asked. He was drifting to his left, sort of boxing Hali in, given how the tiki bar was located at her back.

"Stop right there." Hali sent out one single magical blast in his direction, remaining immovable when it hit the pavement in front of his feet.

Finn looked down, then up, and then back down. He seemed confused. "What was that?"

"I think you should sit with your friend." Hali's tone was no nonsense.

"And if I don't?"

"Then I won't miss with my next blast." She raised her other hand and pointed it at Rip, who looked as if he might get to his feet. "Don't turn this into a thing."

Rip cocked his head, considering, and then unleashed a smile. There was nothing friendly about it. "I think you're under the mistaken impression that we're intent on doing you harm."

"It doesn't matter if my impression is mistaken or not," Hali replied. "I don't trust you. You clearly don't trust me. Don't push me in a corner because you won't like the way I react."

Rip stared at her a beat longer and then motioned for Finn to join him. "You're definitely reading the situation wrong," he said as Finn slumped in a chair. "I don't want to frighten you, however."

"Oh, you misunderstand," Hali intoned. "I'm not frightened. You should be, but I'm not. This is my turf."

Rip let out a snort, and then immediately jerked his eyes to the left. He sensed something, Hali realized. She couldn't be certain what, though.

"Merrow?" she asked, keeping her arms raised as she took a step forward.

Rip's forehead creased in confusion, and he shook his head. "Merrow? I don't understand."

"It's not the merrow," a female voice announced from the shadows.

Hali's insides unclenched as Suki, one of St. Pete Beach's resident sirens, appeared at the edge of the patio. She was without her sisters Helga and Portia, but she was intent as she glanced between Rip and Finn. That told Hali that there was more going on than met the eye.

"Are you okay?" Suki asked after a beat.

"I'm fine," Hali assured her. "My friends just got a little overzealous when paying me a visit."

"They're not your friends." Suki was firm. "Do you even know who they are?"

The question confused Hali, but she considered Suki an ally and refused to keep anything that might be important a secret from her. "Shark shifters. Rip and Finn."

"Wow. Your parents showed real imagination with those names," Suki drawled.

"I thought the sirens in this area were hands off," Rip growled, his words laced with accusatory contempt. "That's what we were told."

"Hali handles the beach," Suki replied. "We handle the waters. We sensed you moving in several nights ago. Your presence hasn't gone unnoticed, and we work together as a team when necessary. I felt you when I was out in the surf just now, and your intentions didn't feel honorable."

"Oh, so you can feel intentions now?" Finn challenged. "Since when is that a siren thing?"

"You would be surprised." Suki's gaze was steady when it landed on Hali. "We've been patrolling closer to the shore for the past two weeks. The merrow are darting in and out. I wanted to make sure your new friends weren't tied to them."

"What do you mean by merrow?" Rip demanded. "Are you talking about a real merrow, or is this just another case of a mermaid pretending to have more power than is possible?"

"They're real merrow," Hali replied. "Like ... bad. They're bad creatures."

"And what do they want with you?" Rip sounded accusatory.

"That is the question of the week," Hali replied dryly. "We don't know. They seem to want to claim some dominion over the beach. They offered to give me Tampa in exchange for St. Pete," she explained to Suki.

"I'm sure I can imagine how that went down." Suki tapped her bottom lip. "They're not to be trusted."

"Real merrow definitely aren't to be trusted," Finn agreed.

"You two aren't to be trusted either," Suki added, glaring at the shark shifters in turn. "I know your reputation."

"What reputation?" Rip was suddenly innocence and light. "I have no idea what you're talking about."

"Oh, whatever." Suki shook her head. "You suck people in, offering them money for their dreams. Then you crush the dreams. You don't belong here."

"We're not planning on staying long term," Rip assured her. "We're only here for a few days."

"You don't belong here at all." Suki was firm. "Our waters are not for you."

"We're not on the water right now," Finn pointed out.

Suki blinked twice and then turned her attention back to Hali. "They're not to be trusted." She was so adamant, it gave Hali pause.

"Like you are?" Rip shot back. "You're a siren. You lure

men to their deaths and use their life essence to bolster your own. You're not exactly trustworthy either."

"You're talking about the sirens of old," Suki countered. "That has not been our way for a very long time. We're not to be trifled with though."

"We're not either."

Hali was dumbfounded as she watched the two sides spar. Suki wasn't one for issuing empty threats. She had no idea what the shark shifters were capable of, however. If it came to a fight, which side would win? It was hard to ascertain. Before she could comment on the strange conversation, Gray appeared on the sidewalk. He'd obviously picked up on the fact that Hali was no longer alone because he arrived on a jog.

"Well, this is an interesting group," he said as he took in all the faces. "What's going on here?"

"Nothing," Rip replied hurriedly, suddenly showing deference to Gray. "We were just hoping for a drink. Your girlfriend told us she wasn't open, so we're heading down the beach."

"Uh-huh." Gray didn't look convinced. He shifted his gaze to Suki. "I haven't seen you in a few weeks. How go things on the water?"

"They're busier than usual," Suki replied, casting a dark look at the shifters. "I don't want to get into Hali's business— she's quite adept at taking care of herself—but these two were trying to box her in when I arrived. It's something I feel you should be made aware of."

Gray's eyes darkened to dangerous slits. "Is that so?"

Hali was at her limit. She grabbed the money envelope from inside the tiki bar and slammed the door shut, going through the motions of locking the space in exaggerated fashion. "Everything is fine," she assured Gray when she was finished, clutching the envelope under her arm. "It's not a big deal."

"It sounds like a big deal." Gray's voice was positively dripping with anger. "Just for the record, you're not going to want to go near her again," he said to Rip. "I'm being serious. I'll tear your head off and use it as a beach ball if you try."

"Ah, you have to love testosterone," Hali muttered, eliciting a smirk from Suki.

"That's not what this is," Gray countered. "You were here alone, minding your own business. It's not okay for them to do ... whatever it is they were trying to do."

"I think they were posturing for your benefit rather than mine," Hali replied. "It doesn't matter though. I had the situation completely under control. I don't need you to throw down to protect my honor. Although, if you want to rip off your shirt and flex for me when we get back to my place, I wouldn't be opposed to that."

Despite his agitation, Gray mustered a smile. "I think that can be arranged." He held out his hand to her. "We'll just leave the three of you to your conversation."

"That's wise," Suki encouraged. "We have some things to discuss. For example, I'm almost positive our visitors don't realize that you're not the only paranormal superheroes on the block. I can't wait to inform them about the vampire that hangs around looking for bad people to feed off of either."

Rip swallowed hard. "You have a vampire on the beach? How is that even possible?"

"Not everything in the real world works as it does in movies," Suki replied. "Vampires are resilient creatures. This one, the one who rules the blood of St. Pete, is extremely fond of Hali. I bet you didn't know that either."

"Not so much," Rip acknowledged.

"Well, then we definitely have things to talk about." Suki slowly lifted her eyes to Gray and Hali. "Have a good night. I'll take it from here."

Hali wanted to press the issue, but she didn't. Whatever plans Suki had for the shark shifters, that was her business.

Hali just wanted them to back off so she could focus on the trivia contest. That was her biggest concern right now.

"How does Chinese sound?" Gray asked as he led Hali away from the tiki hut. "I was thinking we could have it delivered."

"It sounds divine. You're such a good provider."

He kissed the tip of her nose before casting one more look over his shoulder. He wasn't done with the shark shifters. Not by a long shot. "And don't you forget it."

FOURTEEN

Hali and Gray talked about the weird interaction between the shark shifters and the siren before falling into bed. Neither one of them understood the intricacies of their relationship, but it was obvious that something was going on beyond what they were privy to.

The next morning, they showered together, laughed a lot, and then headed out for breakfast with her family. It was a weekly event. Gray had gone once before but begged off since that initial visit. There was no getting out of it this morning, however.

"If they don't see you at least once a month, they're going to think I'm making you up," Hali explained as he navigated the streets of Tampa in his truck.

"Have you made up boyfriends before?" he challenged. "Why would they think that?"

Hali averted her eyes so she was looking out the window. "I have no idea."

Gray didn't believe her. "Oh, come on," he complained. "There's a story there. I can tell."

She blew out a sigh, annoyance obvious. "Fine. When I

was fifteen, I wasn't developing as quickly as the other girls. Things were just lagging." She motioned toward her breasts.

Gray grinned but didn't respond. He could tell he was going to like this story.

"All the other girls had dates for the sophomore fall dance, and I didn't, so I might—I stress *might*—have made up a story about having a boyfriend from a different town." Hali sucked in a breath. "I thought they would just accept the story and let it go. They didn't, though, and they asked my parents about it. Of course, Mom and Dad knew I was lying and said as much, and it's been a family joke ever since.

"When I dated, even well into my twenties, they would always ask if my boyfriend was real or fake," she continued. "It's irritating because I was only fifteen. I don't think that should still be held against me."

"Aw." Gray reached over and collected her hand, giving it a squeeze. "I'm sorry that happened to you. I'm sure you were an adorable teenager."

"That's the point. I didn't want to be adorable. I wanted to be someone other people wanted."

The statement was like a fist around Gray's heart, and he didn't like the feeling that he was suddenly being squeezed. "I want you." His voice was soft but sincere. "I've wanted you since I first laid eyes on you."

Hali managed a smile. "I wanted you too, even though I thought there was a chance you were a psycho."

Gray laughed, as he was certain she'd intended. "Being a teenager is rough," he acknowledged. "It's one of the hardest ages for a reason. It wasn't that those guys back then didn't want you. They just weren't smart enough to know what they were missing."

"That's some roundabout thinking there."

Gray pulled into the Waverly driveway and put his truck in park before turning to face her. "It's the truth. You are magical, Hali. You brighten up my life in a way I didn't know was possible. You can't cling to things that happened as a teenager though. That life is so far removed from this one that they shouldn't be considered linked. You just need to be happy about who you are now, because she's the best person I know."

Hali unfastened her seatbelt, then leaned over to hug him. "You're really good at saying exactly what it is that I need to hear."

"I adore you," he replied simply, his hands going over her back. "More than you can possibly understand." He gave her a soft kiss, was about to go in for a longer one, and then frowned when he caught a hint of movement out of the corner of his eye.

When he turned, he found Hali's father, Steve, watching them with his arms folded over his chest. He didn't look happy.

"I don't think your dad likes me," Gray lamented, sucking in a breath.

Hali followed his gaze, her lips curving into a smirk. "Don't worry. He's all bark and no bite."

Growing up in a pack, Gray had learned that bark wasn't necessarily better than bite. Some words hurt more than deeds. "I guess I have some work to put in."

"My father is going to like you once he wraps his head around how much I like you," Hali promised. "Don't worry about it."

Gray let loose a sigh but nodded. "Here's hoping."

"It will be fine." She patted his hand. "Come on. I'm looking forward to pancakes."

Gray was resigned as he got out of the truck and stood toe to toe with Steve. "Hello, Mr. Waverly." He extended his hand in perfunctory fashion. "It's great to see you."

Steve didn't look wowed with the greeting. There was no

smile to welcome Gray. Instead, he focused on his daughter. "I wasn't certain you would come. You've been quiet the past two weeks."

"That's because she has a boyfriend," Hali's sister, Annie, called out from the front porch. Gray hadn't even seen her standing there. "He's so much better than all her imaginary boyfriends too." Annie smiled at Gray and waved. "Welcome back. We were getting worried when you missed the last few breakfasts."

"Yeah, we thought Hali hired you for one date and then planned to make up stories about you going forward," her brother, Jesse, called out as he joined Annie. For once, he didn't have his phone in his hand. "That was cute when she was a kid. It wouldn't be cute now though. Just pathetic."

"Uh-huh." Gray let loose a breath. The Waverly family was so different from his own. They loved Hali. How could they not? They were hard on her though. It was simply in an amused sort of way. His family had been silent, rigid even. Sure, he and Rusty were rambunctious on their own. When their parents were around, however, there wasn't much fun to be had. The Waverly family was completely different from what he was used to.

Hali was sheepish when she moved to the front of the truck to join him. "Told you."

"I don't care that you had a fake boyfriend," he promised. "I'm just glad I get to be your real boyfriend." He kissed her forehead. When he looked up, he found Steve eyeing him with fresh interest. "I'm sorry I missed the last few breakfasts." Surprisingly, he realized he meant it, if only for Hali's benefit. "I wanted to give Hali the time I thought she needed to be alone with her family. It's come to my attention that was a mistake. It won't happen again."

Steve's eyebrows hopped, and he slid a glance toward

Annie and Jesse before focusing on Gray again. "We're making pancakes. Joyce will be thrilled to see you."

"She was afraid you were imaginary too," Jesse offered.

Gray frowned. Now wasn't the time to lose his cool, but his irritation couldn't be contained. "Well, I assure you I'm not imaginary." He slipped his arm around Hali's waist and anchored her to his side. "Did someone mention pancakes?" he asked when nobody responded.

"Absolutely." Steve bobbed his head and started for the house. "We have many different types of pancakes."

"Awesome."

THEY'D ONLY BEEN IN A RELATIONSHIP FOR A FEW weeks and yet Hali could read Gray better than she could almost anyone. He kept close to her side as they walked through the house, but there was a protective vibe being projected whenever somebody said something aimed at messing with her. When Gray excused himself to go to the bathroom, Hali took the opportunity to admonish her family.

"Can you guys not give him a hard time?" she complained, shaking her head as she washed blueberries at the sink. "He's not used to this sort of thing. He doesn't get that you're just giving me a hard time because you think it's funny. He's constantly having to stop himself from jumping to my defense."

"I thought he had siblings," Joyce argued as she whisked the batter. "That means he should be used to stuff like this."

"He is, to some extent. He and Rusty are close, and they give each other a hard time. He's estranged from his parents, though. It's a difficult situation. Can you please not be all ... *you* ... when he's around? I don't want him to be uncomfortable."

"I didn't realize we were acting a certain way," Steve countered. "I thought we were just being ourselves. I'm sorry he doesn't like us."

"Don't." Hali extended a warning finger. "He likes you fine. He's just nervous. He can't help himself. Don't give him a hard time for no reason. I don't like it, and I think he's going to be around for a good long while, so maybe you can give him a break for me, huh?"

Joyce's eyes sparkled. "Does that mean you're getting married?" She looked beyond hopeful.

"Mother, we've been dating for three weeks," Hali replied pointedly. "I think that's a premature discussion."

"Sometimes when you know, you know."

And, because she didn't disagree, Hali opted to skirt the question. "Let's just settle for having a good breakfast, huh?" She pinned her father with a pointed look. "And not giving Gray a hard time."

"I'm your father, Hali," he replied, not missing a beat. "It's my job to give him a hard time. I would be derelict in my duties if I didn't mess with him at least a little." He blinked several times, but when she didn't relent, he sighed. "Fine. I think he's a little big to be your boyfriend, though. Aren't you worried he could crush you?"

Hali was officially scandalized. "Dad!"

Gray picked that moment to return to the kitchen. One look at his face told Hali he'd heard at least some of the conversation in his absence. *Damn that wolf hearing!*

"Hi." Hali beamed at him. "Do you want to help me wash blueberries?"

Gray managed a quick smile. "Sure." He moved to her and watched as she dumped the berries into a colander. This really wasn't a two-person job, but Hali wanted him close. "How are things with the landscaping business?" he asked Steve for lack of anything better to talk about.

"They're good," Steve replied. He seemed unsure what to

do with his hands. Gray was both taller and broader, and Hali's father didn't seem to know how he should react to the interloper at family breakfast. "How are things in the private investigator business?"

Gray shrugged as he turned on the water to wash the blueberries. "I've taken on a client that's keeping me at Paradise Lodge all week," he replied.

Steve's eyes narrowed. "What sort of client requires that sort of work?"

"He's one of the big figures in the trivia contest," Gray replied. "Unfortunately, he has a reputation as a ladies' man, and it's my job to make sure he doesn't get into trouble. So far, he hasn't been too bad."

"He hasn't been all that good either," Hali argued as she shook the colander to get rid of the excess water. "He's kind of full of himself. He's charming too, though, so you don't necessarily hate him."

Jesse, who had plopped down at the table, looked up from his phone. "You're not talking about Dominic Lawson, are you?"

Surprise registered on Gray's face. "How do you know that name?"

"He's a big deal." Excitement flushed Jesse's features. "He hangs around in the gaming lounge occasionally. I was hoping he would pop in when I heard he was in town, but he's been quiet. The others haven't been quiet, but he hasn't uttered a peep."

Hali's forehead creased as she shifted to regard her brother. "I'm confused," she admitted. "Why would a D-level celebrity be hanging out in your gaming rooms?"

Jesse shot her an admonishing look. "Don't say it like that. The Bard's Bath is more than just a gaming room."

Hali darted a look toward Gray and found his lips twitching. "What's The Bard's Bath?" she demanded.

"That's the online hot tub we all get into a couple times a week. We talk about our days. Dominic is a regular visitor."

"So, a bunch of grown men—"

"And women," Jesse interrupted. "It's not a sausage fest or anything. It's not weird."

"Of course it's not weird," Hali drawled. "Why would I possibly think it's weird?" She rolled her eyes. "So, a bunch of grown men and women get into a virtual hot tub and talk about their problems. And Dominic is a part of this."

"A lot of people follow the trivia circuit," Jesse argued. "I mean ... they are elite athletes after all."

Gray's shoulders jerked. "Athletes?"

"Don't bother." Steve waved a dismissive hand. "I've explained to him more times than I can count that actual sweat has to be present for something to be considered an athletic event. He disagrees."

"And I'm right." Jesse was smug. "There are different types of athletes. Like, for example, professional eaters are athletes."

"Those people in hotdog eating contests?" Gray queried.

"Of course a dude with muscles would say it like that," Jesse complained. "You're not fooling anybody, man. I know from reading books and stuff that all those muscles you hide behind are really a cover because you're insecure with women. If you need a tip on how to romance my sister—not in a gross way or anything because then I'll have to kill you—I'm your man."

Hali had to press her lips together to keep from laughing at Gray's confused expression.

"I'll take it under advisement," Gray said finally, shaking his head. "Tell me about the people who hang out in this virtual hot tub with you."

"Wait." Hali held up a hand to interject herself into the conversation before it could go any further. "Just out of curiosity, are you all naked in this hot tub?"

If looks could kill, Jesse would've knocked Hali flat with a set of laser eyes. He glared at her before making an exaggerated clucking sound with his tongue. "Don't be ridiculous," he seethed. "Everybody is dressed as their avatar from the game. If your avatar has a special swim outfit—which mine does—then you dress in that. Nobody is naked. Don't be gross."

"Just checking," Hali muttered.

Gray smirked, his hand automatically going to Hali's back. "What does Dominic say in this group?"

"He hasn't been there in almost two weeks," Jesse replied, his disappointment at the development obvious. "It's a total bummer. Some of the others have been there though."

"The other contestants?" Hali was confused again. "I didn't realize your gaming room was such a happening place."

"There are a few contestants," Jesse replied. "Like David Kyle Hamburg. He hangs around all the time. He wears a Speedo, and there's no way his real junk is as big as his fake junk because that would make him a porn star, but that's neither here nor there."

Hali and Gray exchanged another look and waited for Jesse to continue.

"It's the sharks that have been stealing the show lately," Jesse continued, not missing a beat. He enjoyed being the center of attention.

"The sharks?" Gray interjected, his interest piqued.

"Yeah. They're shifters who can turn into sharks. It's weird." Jesse looked momentarily lost in thought and then shook his head as he emerged from his reverie. "Anyway, they appeared in the hot tub about a week before Dominic made his last appearance. They're big talkers, but people are more interested in Dominic than them."

Hali licked her lips, debating, and then asked the obvious question. "Their names aren't Rip and Finn, are they?"

"No." Jesse shook his head. "Sir Ripthon and King Finn of the Plains."

Hali waited, but Jesse obviously didn't see why his correction was significant. "Uh-huh. So, it's Rip and Finn."

"Huh. I guess it is." Jesse was perplexed. "I didn't even put that together. How did you know their names?"

"Let's just say that I've had the pleasure of meeting them in person and leave it at that for now," Hali replied. "What are they doing in your hot tub? And if it's something gross, please don't answer."

"I've already told you it's not a gross thing," Jesse protested. "It's just a hanging out thing. As for what they're doing, they're basically taking bets. Everybody is going in big on Dominic. This is his tournament, and everybody knows it. The sharks say that if everybody puts money down on Dominic, however, a lot of people are going to lose money because there are plenty of other contestants who can win. Nobody believes them."

Hali didn't realize she was leaning into Gray until his arm pulled taut and pressed her to his side. They were both clearly thinking the same thing.

"Is something wrong?" Steve asked, obviously picking up on the change in his daughter's demeanor.

"I don't know if 'wrong' is the word I would use to describe what's happening," she hedged. "Things aren't necessarily going well though."

"Meaning what?" Steve glanced between them. "Is something bad happening out at that resort? I knew it was a mistake for you to move out there full-time. Maybe you should come home."

The look Hali shot her father promised that was never going to be a possibility. "I'm fine," she said. "It's just ... there have been a few new faces around the resort because of the trivia contest. It's not a big deal."

Steve didn't look convinced. "I haven't said anything about the witch stuff. I haven't complained that your new boyfriend is the size of an NFL guard. I don't like the idea of you being in trouble, though, Hali. You're my baby."

"Actually, I'm your baby," Jesse argued.

"Yes, but she's the baby I actually care about," Steve fired back. "You still live under this roof. I don't have to worry about you because the only people you talk with are on the computer. Your sister is a different story. She's vulnerable out there."

"Oh, geez, Dad," Hali complained. "I'm not vulnerable. I'm perfectly capable of taking care of myself."

"Besides," Annie added. "You heard Gray. He's shacking up with Hali at the resort this week." She ran an appraising look up and down his body. "I'm pretty sure she's in solid hands."

Hali jabbed a finger toward her sister. "Get your own boyfriend. As for my safety, I'm fine. I wish you would stop worrying about me."

"I can't help it." Steve looked pained. "You're the most independent of all my children. That means I worry about you the most."

"Well, you shouldn't." Hali was firm. "I can take care of myself. Besides, there's nothing bad happening." She tried to not think about the bombs. "Everything is fine. Trust me."

"We trust you," Joyce sang out. "We're also glad you finally got a boyfriend who isn't imaginary. I think things are finally looking up for you."

Hali let out a sigh, defeated. "They are, Mom. And Gray is definitely not imaginary."

"Definitely not," Gray agreed, pressing an absent kiss to the top of her head. The gears in his mind were already working overtime. "So, how about those pancakes?" he prodded after a few seconds of silence. "I hate to eat and run, but I think that's exactly what I'm going to have to do. I need to get back to the resort."

Hali nodded in agreement. She was right there with him. "Let's get to the eating, huh? I think it's going to be a long day."

FIFTEEN

"What do you think?" Hali asked Gray when they were back in his truck and headed toward Paradise Lodge.

"I think your brother needs to get off his lazy butt and stop playing so many video games," Gray replied, his gaze on the traffic.

"Not about *that*. That's a given. About the shark shifters being in the room talking to everybody. It sounds like they want Dominic to lose, right?"

"Or they want Dominic to win and don't like all the people betting on him because it's going to skew the results away from an outcome that's favorable to them."

Hali took a moment to consider it. "I guess that's possible," she said finally. "Why would they go to a gaming room like that, though?"

"I don't know why anybody hangs out in a virtual hot tub when there are real hot tubs out there."

"Jesse's nervous around real people. He can't help himself. He gets anxiety."

Gray arched an eyebrow. "Since when do you stand up for

your brother? You're usually the one telling him to get a job and get out of the house."

"And I stand by that. He should totally get a job and get out of my parents' house. They infantilize him to the point where he's going to be poison to anybody who ever wants to take him on as a husband. He definitely needs to move."

"Hmm." Gray was noncommittal.

"Speaking of, can you believe they wanted me to move back in with them?" Hali demanded, horrified at the memory. "Like that's ever going to happen."

Gray chuckled. "Your family loves you, Hali. They just want to take care of you. That's not a bad thing."

"You heard us though when you went to the bathroom." It wasn't a question. "I know you did."

"You're worried that I'm not going to get along with your family," Gray surmised. "That's not something you can just swallow and accept. I get it. It's okay though. I like them. I'm just not always comfortable around happy families."

"You have Rusty." Hali was insistent. "I know your parents are jerks, but Rusty is great." She reached over and wrapped her fingers around his wrist. "You can be part of my family too."

His heart turned over like a struggling engine at her sincere words. "I want to be with you. I know your family is part of the deal. I like them. Sure, your father is still putting me through my paces, but I'm okay with it.

"I like that he's so protective of you," he continued. "I didn't realize that my absence at family breakfast was going to be such a big deal. I'm truly sorry."

"You don't have to come." Hali was earnest. "I don't want you to be uncomfortable."

"I wasn't uncomfortable. It's just ... that's your family time. I still have time with just Rusty alone. I thought it was like that, somehow necessary for you guys to keep your balance. I'm starting to see that I might've been wrong about that."

Hali sat for a moment, debating. Family matters *were* important. She wouldn't let the bad blood he had with his parents turn into uncertainty for them as a couple, however.

"I think the problem is that I want to fix things for you," she admitted out of the blue. "I want you to have a happy relationship with your parents because it seems so normal. You didn't have the same normalcy I did, though, so it throws you. I don't want it to become a thing."

"It won't." Gray reached over and squeezed her knee. "My parents are not a part of my life, and I'm okay with it. I have my brother. I have you." He grinned. "I just need time to figure out your family because I'm not used to being loved and supported like that."

Hali hated that he could say that and mean it. "I'm so sorry."

"Don't be, baby." His tone was husky. "I like your family. I wish I could give your brother a kick in the butt, but I like them."

"Jesse isn't so bad," Hali insisted. "He has a good heart. He just hasn't found his way yet. He will. I have faith."

Gray nodded. "Either way, he gave us a lead today without even realizing it."

"Yeah. That was weird." Hali rolled her neck. "We're looking for the shark shifters when we get back, right?"

"Oh, most definitely." Gray was decisive when bobbing his head. "I have some questions for them."

"Me too."

"As for your family, I need you not to worry. I truly do like them. We just need to get comfortable around one another. Everything is going to be okay. I promise."

Hali looked placated by his words, which was enough for him. For now, at least. "Let's find those shark shifters," he said.

"This time, they're not leaving without providing the answers we need. I'm sick of playing defense on this one."

"I'm right there with you. I'm going to punch those jerks in the gills if they try to run."

"I'm looking forward to that."

He wasn't the only one.

HALI CHECKED IN AT THE BAR LONG enough to tell Kendra she would be on her own, and then she and Gray headed to the beach. It was a beautiful morning, not too hot as of yet, but the humidity was high, and there was no doubt things would turn steamy in the next two hours.

"I don't see the shifters, but I see the sirens," Gray noted, pointing. "It looks like Suki is talking to Brandon."

Hali nodded. "Then let's head over there."

Gray was already moving. "Yeah. I want to talk to Brandon again anyway."

"You mean Bod?" Hali's tone was teasing.

"I cannot call him Bod. To me, he's always going to be Brandon, the kid who liked to wipe boogers on other kids."

Hali's nose wrinkled. "That's such a guy thing. Jesse did that to us when he was a kid. Annie and I were teenagers, and Jesse would chase us with boogers when we didn't pay enough attention to him. It's so gross."

"As much as I want to give Jesse grief, that *is* typical boy behavior." Gray smirked. "Rusty and I used to do it to each other too. At a certain age, it's frowned upon, however. Brandon kept doing it well into middle school."

"I'm guessing he didn't have a lot of girlfriends."

"No."

"That probably explains why he surrounds himself with women now."

"I find the whole Brotherhood of the Setting Sun thing

concerning," Gray admitted. "I mean, it has the potential to go sideways."

Hali didn't disagree. "So far, what he's doing is mostly harmless. The women come and go. If he does take it to the next level, then we'll have to step in. For now, he's not one of my top ten concerns on this beach."

"Agreed." Gray squared his shoulders when approaching the group. "Good morning."

Bod shifted to see who was encroaching on his space and scowled. "I'm not doing anything."

Gray chuckled. "I didn't say you were, Brandon. Besides, if you tried recruiting these guys, I have no doubt they would handle the situation themselves."

"He needs a bath," Helga complained, wrinkling her nose and waving her hand for emphasis. "You can smell him from two miles away. It's disconcerting. There's no way we would even consider joining his harem."

"From the water, it smells like a corpse," Suki explained.

"A bloated corpse that's gone undiscovered for a week," Portia muttered.

Hali smiled because she knew it was better to be friendly with the sirens than to be looked upon as an enemy, but she only liked Suki when it came to their particular trio. Portia and Helga were standoffish. That didn't mean she wanted to argue with them.

"Maybe you should hit the shower up by the resort," she suggested to Bod. "There's an outdoor faucet for those coming in from the beach. It's meant to handle the sand issue, and rinse saltwater, but I'm sure if you were to take some shampoo and body wash up there in the mornings, nobody would give you grief."

Bod didn't look thrilled with the suggestion. "What's wrong with being natural?"

"You just heard what's wrong," Gray snapped. "You smell like death. Why must you torture us all?"

"Whatever." Bod folded his arms across his chest. "I don't need this abuse."

Hali smirked before turning to Suki. "We're looking for the shark shifters. You didn't kill them last night or anything, did you?"

"No, but I wanted to." Suki's smile was feral. "They're not good people."

"We're not under any delusion that they are," Hali assured her. "We need to talk to them though. It seems they've been trying to influence bets on the trivia contest, and not in a manner that I could've foreseen. They've been hanging around in gaming rooms online and pushing people to bet on people other than Dominic Lawson."

Suki's forehead filled with contemplation wrinkles. "That's interesting. I don't know who Dominic is, but the fact that they're trying to control the betting activity is hardly surprising. They're in big trouble financially if the rumors are to be believed."

Gray straightened. "Is that so? What have you heard?"

"There's a reason they don't come up here very often," Portia replied. "We control these waters and don't want them here."

"Because they're shark shifters?" Hali demanded. "Why don't you like them?"

"It's not that they're shifters," Suki interjected quickly.

"Speak for yourself," Portia muttered on a pout.

Suki continued as if her sister siren hadn't spoken. "We're fine with shifters." She pointed the statement toward Gray. "It's their behavior that's the problem."

"They hunt for sport," Helga complained. "That's just so ... tacky."

Hali glanced at Gray for clarification.

"Hunting for sport is frowned upon," he explained quickly. "Hunting to survive is one thing. It's necessary. Killing just to kill though, no matter your pack or genetic makeup, it's just not supposed to be a thing."

"It's a human thing," Portia argued. "Humans kill just to kill. We're supposed to be better than that."

"Huh." Hali was thoughtful. "I guess I never thought about it that way."

"Hunting to feed your people is fine," Suki said hurriedly. "It's the waste of a life that we don't like."

"And the shark shifters are wasting life?"

"That's what they do," Portia replied. "Years ago, we had a meeting of minds with them, if you will. They're allowed in our waters if they promise to do no damage. We've seen damage though."

"And that's why I stayed to talk to them last night," Suki volunteered. "We reminded them of our agreement."

"That sounds fair," Gray noted. "How did they respond?"

"They promised to be better. We will see."

"But they're in financial trouble?" Hali prodded.

"That's the rumor," Helga replied. "They keep their business confined to Treasure Island mostly, so we've only heard rumors. Supposedly, their father—they're brothers if you didn't already figure that out—bought some big resort there, and he's practically run it into the ground. They're trying to bring in fast money to shore up their finances or risk losing the resort. We heard they're quite desperate now."

Gray rubbed his chin. "That might explain why they're trying to rig the bets on the tournament. If they have a way to ensure that Dominic wins, they're going to want bets on other contestants."

"Jesse made it sound like Dominic is the favorite," Hali noted.

"Yeah." Gray absently moved his hand to her back. "I'm guessing Rip and Finn don't like that."

"I wonder if they're concerned enough to try to influence which questions are being asked at the tournament," Hali mused. "I mean ... they might not be smart enough to realize that there's no influencing the tournament from that angle."

"I would like to hear their feelings on the subject," Gray confirmed. "I don't suppose you guys know where we can find them, do you?" he asked the sirens.

Suki shared a look with Portia and then forced a smile. "They've been spending a lot of time in the smoking area off the main resort. You know that area with the benches and the fan? If they're not there, they'll show up within the hour."

Hali smiled in thanks. "I think we're going to have that talk with them sooner rather than later."

"It sounds prudent," Suki agreed. "Let us know if you need any help later in the day. In this particular matter, we're willing to play on your team."

"Speak for yourself," Portia grumbled. "I'm my own team."

"I'll keep you updated," Hali promised. "We all want to keep the beach safe."

"Yes. That includes from the merrow," Suki supplied. "That's a concern for another day though."

HALI AND GRAY WALKED TO THE MAIN resort building together, Hali waving to various workers as they made the trek. Gray smiled as he watched her interact, his chest warming.

"You know everybody here," he noted as they cut down the hallway that led to the exit by the smoking area. "You make a point to greet everybody."

"It takes very little effort to do the small things," Hali

replied. "I would rather be the good part of someone's day than the bad part, even if I don't realize when I'm the bad part."

"You're always the best part of my day," he announced as they walked into the blooming heat. "Even before we got together, you were always the best part of my day. That realization is what made me ask you out."

"So sweet," a male voice drawled as Hali grinned at him.

Her smile disappeared in an instant as she swiveled to take in Rip and Finn. They were indeed sitting on separate benches in the smoking area, just as Suki suggested. To Hali, that meant the sirens were keeping an even closer eye on the shifters than she'd realized.

"We're definitely sweet," Gray agreed as he moved into the small rectangular area. He glanced around, then directed Hali to the open bench. He didn't want her in striking distance should their questions irritate the shifters. "I'm going to get straight to the point," he said when he and Hali had sat, shoulder to shoulder. He didn't want to come across as intimidating, but he refused to present himself as meek either. He needed a tempered approach.

At least to start.

"By all means," Rip replied, leaning back as if he didn't have a care in the world. "Get straight to the point."

"It's come to our attention that your family might be in financial trouble," Gray replied. "We also know you've been in some of the virtual gaming lounges pushing people to bet for individuals other than Dominic, who is considered the favorite. We want to know if your financial need is dire enough to have you trying to influence what questions might be asked at the tournament."

Rip's mouth dropped open.

"In other words," Gray continued, not missing a beat. "We want to know if you killed Brian Parker because you thought that meant you could somehow influence the outcome of the tournament."

Hali was impressed. When Gray said he was going to get to the heart of matters right away, she had no idea how accurate that statement would turn out. She was impassive as he questioned the shifters, but she was smiling inside.

"Is that what you really think about us?" Rip demanded when he found his voice.

"We're just trying to find some answers," Gray replied.

"Well, great for you I guess." Rip shook his head and then blew out a sigh. "It's true we need a few events to go our way. Our father has made a rather grave error with an investment. We're not stupid though. How is killing a tournament worker going to ensure that our preferred contestant wins?"

"He handled the question bundles," Gray replied.

"That doesn't matter. If he'd been killed while carrying the bundles, new bundles would've been generated. If he didn't have the bundles on him, then there's literally nothing that can be done. We're not idiots."

Gray stared at Rip hard, as if trying to mentally break him. After several seconds, he leaned back and stretched his long legs out in front of him. "It doesn't make sense," he conceded finally. "None of it makes sense. That being said, you guys have been acting out of sorts. Last night, you tried to mess with my girlfriend. You must understand why I'm suspicious."

"We didn't try to mess with her for the reasons you think," Finn argued. "We were trying to get answers about you."

"We just went about it in the wrong way," Rip added. "In our shiver, women defer to men. We thought she would be able to give us information on you, on your preferences and whether you'll be joining a shiver or not."

Gray's forehead creased. "What the hell is a shiver?"

"It's a pack of sharks," Hali replied before they could. "Sometimes people mistakenly call them a pod, like with whales, but it's a pack of sharks. It was one of Lana's fun facts a few weeks ago."

"Oh." Gray rubbed his cheek. "I guess that's kind of cool. If you have questions about my preferences and plans, however, you need to ask me. You don't go after my girlfriend."

"We weren't going after her," Rip insisted. "We just ... wanted to get a feel for her."

"It's rare that we spend time with witches," Finn explained. "Your union is ... unique."

"How so?" Hali queried.

"Well, first off, he's half wolf and half shark. I'm sure that there have been others who can claim that distinction, but not recently. He has his foot in two worlds and his heart in another, and that's fascinating to us."

"When you add in the witch factor, your children could be something entirely new," Rip added.

"We're fascinated. We can't help ourselves."

"Try," Gray shot back. "Don't back Hali into a corner ever again. She doesn't need me to protect her—she could've handled you on her own without breaking a sweat—but I'll kill to keep her safe. Make no mistake about it."

Finn turned sheepish. "We really weren't trying to make things difficult for her," he promised. "We went about things the wrong way. We often go about things that way, however, so we really didn't think we were taking liberties with her safety. We apologize."

Gray nodded in acceptance. "Listen, I really don't have my feet in both worlds. My shark side has never been explored. I was raised in the wolf pack. I'm not in that world either though."

"Yes, we know." Now Rip smiled. "You fought the hierarchy and left with your life. It's impressive." He inclined his head toward Hali. "She is impressive too. Together you're—"

"Impressive?" Gray surmised.

"And then some," Rip confirmed. "We can't help being curious."

"That's all well and good," Gray said. "Don't ever threaten her again though. As for any children we have one day—which is far down the line—we're going to raise them how we want to raise them. They won't be pack, and they won't be shiver. They're going to be their own people."

"Fair enough." Rip held up his hands in a placating manner. "We apologize and promise not to get in your way. As for the dead tournament employee, we don't benefit from what happened. Do we want Dominic to win? Yes. We need the bets on other people as well though. We didn't kill that man. There was no profit in it for us."

Gray believed him. "Then there's still another killer out there," he mused as he glanced at Hali. "Who would benefit from that guy's death?"

"That I can't answer." Rip was rueful. "We've talked about it as well. I can't think of a single person who would benefit from his death."

"Well, somebody thought there was something in it for them," Gray argued. "We need to figure out who."

"Good luck with that."

"Thanks. I think we're going to need it."

Sixteen

They had nowhere else to look, so Hali and Gray separated in the lobby. Gray wanted to talk to Dominic, although they both agreed pushing him to give answers on whether he knew about the shark shifters' plot would be a no-win scenario. That left Hali to head to the Salty Cauldron and open it before the next tournament round.

To her surprise, she found Wayne waiting at the back of the bar.

"What's up?" she asked as she looked the flamingo up and down. For once, he didn't appear hungover. That felt like a small miracle despite the dregs of the day descending upon them.

"Why does something have to be up?" he demanded. "Maybe I'm here to do my job. I bet that didn't even cross your mind."

"It didn't," Hali readily agreed. "You've never done your job since I've known you."

"And what tasks have you given me?"

Hali froze. It was a fair question. "Maybe I don't want to give tasks to a drunk," she said finally.

"And maybe I wouldn't get drunk if I had something to do."

She gripped the rag she was holding tighter and then nodded. "Fine. I want you to watch the trivia tournament. If you sniff out anything weird, report back."

"That's it?" Wayne didn't have eyebrows, but Hali got the distinct impression he would be cocking one now if he could.

"We don't know exactly what we're looking for," Hali conceded. "One of the tournament workers is dead. He handled the question bundles. The thing is, he didn't have them on him when he died. They were locked in the hotel safe. So, why kill him?"

"I don't know."

"I don't know either."

"But you think it was one of the contestants?"

Hali shrugged. "We don't know. Maybe. It could've been another worker. Maybe his death had nothing to do with the question bundles and everything to do with some workplace romance gone wrong. I feel in my heart it has something to do with the tournament, however."

Wayne studied her for what felt like a long time and then nodded. "I'll watch for anything weird."

"Thank you." Hali hesitated a beat and then continued. "They're going to do the quarterfinal round first. Then they're changing clothes and doing the semifinal round right after. Lana is still in the running."

"You mean fun fact girl?"

"Yes. Stick close to her. I don't want her becoming a victim in all of this. Whatever is going on, she's innocent. If something happens to her, I'm going to be very upset."

Wayne rolled his eyes but didn't argue. "Fine. I'll watch her. Anybody else you want me to watch?"

"Yes. Dominic Lawson. He'll be coming down with Gray in about twenty minutes. Watch him too."

"And why do we care about him?"

"Because he's at the center of this, whether he realizes it or not. That could make him a victim or a perpetrator. I'm not sure which. I just want him watched."

"Then I'll watch him." Wayne turned to head down to the beach. "For the record, I don't like your boyfriend. He's mean, and he screwed up the good thing we had going."

"You mean the thing where you passed out wherever you wanted and made my life hell?"

"Clearly, you didn't think it was that great, but I did. I guess ... um ... I guess I'm going to have to get used to him though."

"You are." Hali was firm. "He's going to be around."

"Forever?"

Her heart squeezed. "I don't know. I hope so though."

"Something tells me you're going to get what you want."

Hali smiled. "Maybe."

GRAY WAS ANNOYED WITH DOMINIC'S CONSTANT grousing. Sure, the job had turned out to be easier than expected when he'd first heard about Dominic's past. That didn't mean Dominic wasn't a complete and total pain.

"You were paid to be here, right?" Gray demanded as they skirted around a happy couple on the sidewalk. "That means you have to fulfill your obligations and shut up."

Dominic shot him an incredulous look. "Since when is that the rule? I have it on good authority that people talk badly about their jobs no matter what that job is. Like ... people who take photos on cruise ships? They actually complain about it. This is the same thing."

"No, it's not." Gray shook his head. "You basically answer trivia questions for a few hours a day. It's not every day either.

You like trivia as far as I can tell. Your hotel is paid for. Your drinks and food are paid for. You have nothing to complain about."

"What about the fact that you stole the only interesting woman?"

Gray narrowed his eyes. "You're not going to want to go there."

"Yeah, yeah, yeah." Dominic waved off Gray's anger. "I'm just saying that usually the pickings aren't so slim. Apparently, the waters in the Gulf are murky when fishing for women."

Gray didn't crack a smile, but he wanted to. "You are ... just too much. Has anybody ever told you that?"

"Nobody of consequence."

"Well, just keep your head in the game." Gray thought about Rip and Finn and steeled himself for the next part. "You don't ever ... like ... bet on yourself in these tournaments, do you?"

Dominic's mouth dropped open. "Are you serious? That's a surefire way to get yourself tossed from the circuit."

"Have people been caught before?"

"Yeah, and they don't last long if they go that route. It is not the safe way to play."

The statement struck Gray as funny. "You never struck me as a 'safe' guy." He used air quotes and kept his lips firm, so he didn't burst out laughing.

"Maybe not on some things." Dominic was deadly serious now. "When it comes to wrapping Little Dominic and not exposing my back to an enemy, I'm as uptight as the next person. I don't want to lose this gig. I realize how lucky I have it. I play by the rules when it comes to the circuit."

"Okay." Gray nodded. "I'm glad to hear that."

"Nobody is saying I don't, right? I don't want that rumor spreading. I don't like it."

Gray managed to contain his surprise, although just barely.

"I haven't heard any rumors. I do know there are loan sharks in the area." Actual sharks who provided loans, he realized, and bit off another laugh. "I was just curious how all of that worked."

"Nobody with any brains bets on their own tournaments." Dominic was emphatic. "Trust me. They have people undercover and stuff to sniff out when someone is doing something to ruin the integrity of the game. That's not me."

"Okay." Gray forced a smile. "I was just asking."

"Well, it's not me."

Gray watched Dominic lope off to take his seat for the quarterfinals, shaking his head before turning to look at the Salty Cauldron. He caught sight of Hali immediately. She was in the tiki hut mixing drinks, her bottom lip caught between her teeth as she concentrated. She looked intense, and yet he went warm all over when he saw her. There was no hesitation when he started in her direction. He could watch Dominic from the comfort of his regular stool at the tiki bar as easily as another location closer to the stage.

The only regular face he recognized when he sat down was Annabelle. She had her computer out, a pink frozen cocktail half-finished next to her, and seemed to be in a mood.

"Fun fact," Hali said as she handed Gray an iced tea. Her gaze was on Annabelle, so Gray knew whatever she was going to say wouldn't be directed at him. "You typically only breathe out of one nostril at a time."

Annabelle blinked. "Who told you that?"

"Who do you think?" Hali challenged.

Annabelle cracked a smile. "Is that the only one you've got? If I'm being honest, I kind of miss her. She's been caught up with the other contestants. I didn't think I would miss her, but I do. It's annoying."

One look at the set of Hali's jaw told Gray she already knew that which was exactly why she'd dropped the fun fact.

There she was, the woman who kept stealing his heart a little more each passing day, going out of her way for people again. She was absolutely amazing.

"Figs aren't considered vegan because they have dead wasps inside," Hali replied, not missing a beat.

"Gross." Annabelle screwed up her face into an expression of disgust. "Now I'm going to have nightmares."

"Also, Caesar salad was invented in Mexico by an Italian-American man."

"That one I actually find interesting," Annabelle mused.

"There's a holiday dedicated to what would happen if cats and dogs had opposable thumbs," Hali added.

"And we're back to nightmares." Annabelle flashed a cheeky grin. "I'm fine," she said to Hali's unasked question, telling Gray that she too recognized what Hali was doing. "I'm just anxious for things to go back to normal. There are too many people out on the beach midday right now. It's not my favorite event that's ever been held here."

"It won't be long," Hali assured her. "The finals are tomorrow. We can say goodbye to the upheaval then."

"I'm so looking forward to it."

Hali smiled, but it didn't touch her eyes. "Me, too."

THE QUARTERFINALS WENT OFF WITHOUT a hitch, a few more faces—none of whom Hali recognized—being eliminated during the round. When they arranged the contestants for the semifinals, there were only two long tables on the stage. Hali recognized that meant the competition was getting serious.

"You look intent," Mia said as she sat at one of the few open stools near the tiki hut. "Do you always look this intent?"

"Hmm?" Hali dragged her eyes away from the round that

was starting and focused on Mia. She hadn't seen her since the overheating incident days prior. "Oh, one of my regulars has made it to the semifinals." She pointed at Lana. "I'm just saying a little prayer that she somehow makes it to the finals."

Mia chuckled. "She's one of the few locals to hold her own this tournament. It's interesting. Do you know her well?"

"Fairly well," Hali confirmed. "She's in here at least three or four times a week. I think this is where she comes when she wants to socialize."

Mia nodded in understanding. "Some of the contestants we see aren't all that comfortable around people. They like facts and figures. Societal niceties are beyond them."

"Oh, Lana is perfectly pleasant," Hali replied. "She just says nutty things sometimes. She can't help herself. I own a bar, though. I'm used to hearing nutty things. For example, just today I learned that a pod of sharks is called a shiver, and I'm fascinated. Like … who came up with that?"

Mia blinked several times and then lifted one shoulder. "One of life's little mysteries I guess."

Hali was surprised. The woman worked on a trivia tournament circuit. It seemed to her she should be used to hearing fun facts. Even more, Hali had to wonder why she wasn't better at covering when she was bored with a conversation. That had to happen regularly.

"So, what will it be?" Hali asked as she shifted gears.

"Um, how about one of those Mermaid Tail drinks? You can include the alcohol, although I'll deny it if anybody asks. I also wouldn't cry if I could have another bag of ice for my back."

Hali smiled. Perhaps it was the heat throwing Mia off. Some people simply couldn't handle it. She'd seen some horrific responses to the humidity from more than one tourist over the years. "Coming right up." She filled a baggie with ice first and handed it over and then proceeded to blend the

Mermaid Tail drink. At one point, she caught sight of Gray, who had meandered over to the sand to watch the contestants settle in for the semifinals. He caught her looking at him and blew a kiss. Hali's cheeks heated with delight, even though she internally chastised herself for being such a giddy, girly girl.

"You guys are adorable," Mia noted as Hali delivered her drink.

"Who?" Hali asked blankly.

"You and your boyfriend." Mia gestured toward Gray. "Half the people in our group are talking about you. The women are jealous of you, and the men are jealous of him."

"When have they even seen us together?" Hali queried.

"Are you kidding?" Mia barked out a harsh laugh. "You guys are either on the beach together, or in the parking lot together, or having breakfast together. You even go to the smoking area together."

The statement caught Hali off guard. As far as she knew, nobody had seen her and Gray talking with Rip and Finn in the smoking area. None of the guests had passed them during the conversation. None of the workers had gone by. It had just been the four of them.

So how did Mia know about the conversation? It was the only time she and Gray had ever been to the smoking area together as far as she could remember.

"We don't smoke," Hali volunteered quickly. "We were actually doing something else."

"When?" Mia sipped her drink, seemingly confused.

Was she playing a game? Hali couldn't tell. "It doesn't matter." Hali forced a smile she didn't feel. "Are you one of the people who is jealous?"

"Oh, absolutely." Mia bobbed her head. "You guys are amazing together. It's all the little touches that get me."

"Little touches?"

"You know, when he brushes your hair out of your face.

When he moves his hands over your back. He's always trying to hug you. There are even little kisses he deposits on the top of your head. It's the sort of stuff women read romance novels for."

"Really?" Hali was bothered on multiple levels. She and Gray were demonstrative at the bar, but someone would have to be really watching them to pick up on all of those things. So, why was Mia watching them? Was it really jealousy, like she said, or something more? Hali couldn't wrap her head around it. "I guess I didn't realize we were acting like teenagers."

"Oh, it's not that you're acting like teenagers," Mia replied hurriedly. "I wasn't saying that. Teenagers have all this angst driving them. You guys are clearly falling in love with one another in real time. It's lovely. I like it when a couple hasn't been together so long that they're jaded."

"Did someone tell you how long we'd been together?"

"Oh, no." Mia waved her hand. "It's just obvious that it's new. I can't remember the last time I had a new romance. Everything in my life feels old, like it should be fading but hasn't gotten the memo yet."

"That's kind of sad."

"Are you saying everything in your life was rosy before your boyfriend walked into it? If so, then I'm definitely jealous."

"No. I'm not saying that. I guess I just like hearing an outsider's opinion."

"Well, in my opinion, you guys are living the dream. It's absolutely amazing."

"I guess it is."

THE SEMIFINALS WERE TENSE, TO THE POINT where Hali started chewing on her thumbnail because her nerves were shot. She had it gnawed down to the quick when Gray took her hand away from her mouth and held it.

"Don't," he admonished through the tiki hut window. "You're going to make yourself bleed if you're not careful."

"I can't help it." Hali's stomach was a squirming mess of snakes as she watched Lana consider what would be the last question of the round. "She's one right answer away from the final."

Gray chuckled. "You're acting like her mother."

"No, I'm not." Hali scowled at him. "It's just ... this is essentially her dream come true. If she could win, that would be the best thing that ever happened to her up until this point. Her self-esteem would be through the roof."

"She shouldn't have to win a contest to get a self-esteem boost."

"No, but that's who she is. I just want her to get her chance." Hali held her breath as Lana answered.

The announcer, a complete and total tool of a man, beamed at her. "Correct."

The crowd broke into enthusiastic applause as the round was brought to a close and the scores were tallied. Lana's cheeks were red with excitement as the announcer read off the names for the final.

"With that answer, Ms. Silver, you'll be joining our other finalists. Dominic Lawson."

More applause broke out. Dominic didn't look surprised at the announcement. He was too fixated on a bikini-clad young woman in the crowd. She kept jiggling her breasts when jumping up and down in excitement, and it was obvious how Dominic planned to celebrate.

"Cadence Carpenter," the announcer intoned.

For her part, Cadence merely smiled.

"David Kyle Hamburg," the announcer added, causing the human thumb to beam.

"And last, but certainly not least, Cathy Thompson," the announcer added.

"I don't know the last one well," Gray noted as he leaned in closer to Hali. "Do you know that woman?"

Hali shook her head. "I think Dominic mentioned the name when he was giving us the rundown of all the players the other day," Hali replied. "He said Cathy was competition."

"Still, there are only five of them in the final. Lana has as much of a chance as anyone."

Hali smiled when she nodded, but there was a niggling sense of dread crawling through her chest. "If something is going to happen, it's going to happen before the final round don't you think?"

Gray hesitated, but not for very long. "Maybe. It's possible that Brian Parker was killed for some other reason. I know we've touched on it, but you don't really seem to be considering it."

"I can't," Hali replied. "It doesn't feel right. I have to go with my gut."

"And what does your gut tell you?"

"That we're not out of this, and now we're on a timetable. Whatever is going to happen is going to happen between now and the start of the finale."

"Okay." Gray sucked in a breath. "Where do you want to look?"

"If I knew that, I wouldn't feel sick to my stomach."

Gray leaned through the opening and pressed a kiss to her cheek. "We'll figure it out."

Hali could only hope that was true.

SEVENTEEN

Lana was so excited about making it to the finals Hali allowed the regulars to stay late and celebrate with her. Annabelle, who was still annoyed because she hated change, made a big show of congratulating her, which had Lana's eyes filling with tears and Annabelle glaring at Hali as if to say, "no good deed goes unpunished."

Gray helped Hali clear the tables once they closed things down. He said he wanted to keep active, but Hali knew better. He was trying to keep her from exhausting her hip. Because she didn't want to fight, she didn't argue when he started wiping down the tables. It was a conversation they would have to have in the future. For now, though, she let it go.

Slowly, the guests started to trickle away. Lana and Annabelle were the last to leave. Even though Hali wanted to celebrate Lana's big triumph, she was ready to call it a night, so when the final two women headed off, she let out a breath.

"I'll check the tables down on the beach," Gray volunteered. He was already heading in that direction. "You stay up there and do what you need to do."

Hali glared at his back, debating if now was the time to

have the argument after all, but it died on her lips when a shadowy figure appeared on the patio. For a moment, she didn't recognize the interloper. Then, when the shadow stepped forward into the limited light and she could make out his features, her insides relaxed enough to have her smiling.

"Hey, Vin," she called out.

Vinson "Vin" Madden was the stereotypical vampire all other vampires hated. He had long dark hair, piercing dark eyes, and he wore full suits in the Florida heat just because he could. He wasn't a regular at Hali's bar, but once every two weeks or so, he appeared when she was cleaning up and got caught up on the gossip. For some reason, Hali was doubly happy to see him tonight.

"Closing up?" Vin asked as he glanced around.

"Yeah, but you're more than welcome to have a drink and watch." Hali went for the liquor stash. "What will it be?"

"Something simple," he replied. "A gin and tonic is fine."

"Are you sure?" Hali made a face. "I can make something in the blender."

"Actually, the gin sounds soothing," Vin said as he sat on one of the stools. "I feel ... *unsettled* ... this evening. I don't want anything too sugary. It makes me jittery."

"Okay." Hali nodded in understanding. "One gin and tonic coming right up." Because she knew he was fussy, she avoided the rail gin and went with the Tanqueray. By the time she dropped the garnish in the glass, Vin was fully comfortable and watching her. "What?" she asked defensively.

"You have something on your mind," he surmised.

"How do you know that?"

"I know you." Vin sipped his cocktail. "Tell me what's going on."

"Actually, we have a few somethings going on," Hali admitted ruefully. She filled Vin in. She could make Gray out as he worked on the beach. She had no doubt he'd caught sight of the vampire. Since they knew each other, however, he didn't come running to Hali's rescue. That was something, she told herself. That was a respite for his busy mind. He didn't always have to worry about her.

"Well, that's interesting," Vin mused when she was finished. "I've been keeping up on the trivia contest this week. I'm glad Lana is doing so well. She deserves to win."

"Everybody loves the underdog," Hali agreed. "She doesn't have the same pedigree as some of the others, though. Like ... Dominic is one of the favorites. All the women love him."

"He's a cupid. That's to be expected."

Hali's eyebrows shot up her forehead. She hadn't mentioned the cupid angle, which meant Vin was doing his own digging on the players for some reason. "You took the time to research the participants?" She pressed her lips together and studied his face, not saying anything else.

"Oh, don't look at me that way," Vin admonished. "I don't really care about the outcome. When a new faction invades my space, however, I like to know who I'm dealing with."

"Okay." Hali held up her hands in mock surrender. "I was just curious."

"No, you're a busybody." Vin shot her a fond smile despite her words. "You've always been a busybody."

"I can't help myself. I never pictured you getting into trivia."

"It's not the trivia," Vin assured her. "It's the new faces. There's an undercurrent of tension rolling up and down this beach right now. Something is going to happen. I can feel it."

Hali hesitated and then rested her hands on the bar counter-top with a nod. "There's a lot going on," she agreed. "The merrow are back."

Vin lifted his chin. "I'd wondered. The sirens have been whispering. It takes something big to get them tittering."

"Actually, I think they're irritated by the shark shifters. They mentioned some sort of agreement that keeps the shifters out of our area. Like ... they mentioned giving Treasure Island to them and keeping St. Pete for themselves."

"I'm not privy to that arrangement," Vin replied. "I'm not surprised though. I'm not all that familiar with shark shifters. The two in question have an interesting reputation, however."

"Meaning what?" Gray asked as he approached with a bag full of garbage. He handed Hali the rag he'd been using to wipe down the tables. "Everything out there is set." He beamed at her.

"That's a convenient way to keep me from having to exhaust myself going out to check, huh?" she said pointedly.

Caught, Gray turned sheepish. "I'm not trying to rule you. I just can't stand when you're in pain."

"I know," Hali replied on a sigh. "It's a bad situation. I'm just not ready."

"And I'm not going to push you before you're ready," Gray promised. "That doesn't mean I won't help if I can help. You need to get used to it."

"We'll talk about it later."

"Okay, but my opinion on the subject is not going to change," Gray said. "I'm going to hold strong on this one."

The way he puffed his chest out made Hali smirk. "We'll talk about it later," she said firmly. "We might even fight about it."

"Good. Then we can make up after." Gray slid onto the stool next to Vin. "I take it Hali has gotten you up to speed on what we're dealing with."

"Mostly," Vin confirmed. He and Gray had a solid relationship. It was nowhere near as tight as the one Hali shared with the vampire, but they liked and respected one another.

They would be allies in tough times if it came to it. "What do you think is going on with the dead man?"

"I honestly don't know." Gray dragged a hand through his hair and let out a breath. "It seems like the fact that he was in charge of handling the questions should somehow play into his death, and yet each lead we chase sends us toward a dead end."

"Okay. Let's break it down." Vin was calm and analytical, something Hali found soothing. "Your dead guy handled the questions. Turns out the questions were computer-generated though. So, even if he'd been carrying the hard copies on his body when he died—which he wasn't—they could've just generated new questions if the first batch had gone missing. So, there really was no edge to be gained for any of the contestants."

"That's a fair assessment," Gray confirmed.

"And yet the betting on this tournament is bound to be irregular," Vin added.

"Because of the shark shifters?" Hali queried.

"I don't know these specific shifters, other than by reputation, but it sounds like they're very intense. They want Dominic to win, so they're in gaming rooms encouraging others to bet on participants other than him. How can they be so certain Dominic is going to win?"

"I don't know." Hali was genuinely baffled. "We asked them if they killed Brian Parker. They said they didn't."

Vin shot Hali an adoring look. "Do you really think that they would admit if they were guilty?"

"No, but I think I would've been able to read them clearly enough to ascertain guilt if it was there," she replied.

"Fair enough. What if they're not the only ones trying to manipulate the betting system though?"

"Who else could it be?" Hali asked blankly.

"You're missing a very big component here," Vin replied.

"You said it wouldn't work for any of the contestants to steal the questions because if the hard copies went missing, they would be replaced, and new questions would be generated."

"That's how it was explained to us," Hali confirmed.

"What happens if someone who works with the tournament takes the questions and doesn't tell anybody?"

Hali stilled. "Oh," she said finally. "You think it was one of the other tournament workers."

"I think the other tournament workers would have access to the safe," Vin confirmed. "At least one other person has to be able to move the questions from the safe, correct? If I'm not mistaken, they've been removing question bundles for the announcer multiple times a day."

Hali's hand flew up, and she smacked herself on the forehead. "Oh, holy hell."

"Yeah." Gray shook his head sheepishly. "How did we miss that?"

"Because we're morons," Hali replied darkly. "We didn't even consider that it could be another tournament employee. The only time we brought them into the equation was when we suggested that Brian might be having an affair with one of them and his death could've been a result of a relationship gone wrong."

"Pretty much," Gray agreed. "We didn't even look at them."

"From your perspective, I can see how that might've happened," Vin replied gently.

"Thanks for that, but it was a mistake on our part." Gray started typing on his phone. "Andrew sent me a breakdown of all the workers. He knew I was sticking close. Let's see what we've got, shall we?"

"You're smarter than both of us combined," Hali said to Vin. "I feel like a bit of an idiot."

"I'm looking in from the outside," Vin replied gently. "It's easier to see the bigger picture from that vantage point. You've been in the thick of things. Have you met any of the other workers?"

"There aren't many of them," Hali replied. "The stage crew, for example, was hired locally. As for tournament workers, there are only three or four of them. There's the announcer." She started ticking the workers off on her fingers. "He seems like a bit of a tool."

"Hal Halverson," Gray said out loud. "That's his name. I have the list up."

"Hal Halverson is a stupid name," Hali complained.

"Totally stupid," Gray readily agreed. "Andrew did some legwork here and left me his notes. It seems Hal has a record, but it's all drunk and disorderly charges. He brings home six figures a year for basically three days of work every other week. He travels with the tournament, and his home base is in Arizona."

"Financial trouble?" Vin queried.

Gray shook his head. "Andrew checked. He's got more than a million in savings. A million bucks doesn't buy what it used to, but he's not in financial trouble as far as I can tell."

"So, let's move on from him," Vin said.

"Yeah. There's Carla Hampton." Gray's full attention was on his screen, and yet he reached over to stroke Hali's forearm as he read. It was an unconscious movement. He simply wanted to touch her. "She's technically what's called the tournament coordinator. I think that makes her the big fish in the little pond."

"I haven't met her," Hali noted. "I have met Mia. She's the assistant tournament coordinator."

"Mia Jankowski," Gray read aloud, bobbing his head. "She's listed here too. Let's focus on Carla first though." He turned his phone screen so Hali could see it. "This is her photo."

Hali studied the woman in question. Hard. Try as she might, she couldn't conjure a single instance where she'd crossed paths with the woman since the tournament had started. "I'm almost positive I haven't seen her."

"I know." Gray looked troubled. "I was just sitting here thinking that. I'm positive I would remember her if she'd been down here."

"Because you think she's hot?" Hali teased.

Gray shook his head. "No, because I've been watching the beach for days at this point. I've been purposely cataloging all the faces. Hers is not a face I've seen."

"I wonder why," Hali replied. "Does Andrew say that he talked to her in his notes?"

"He says that she didn't answer her phone when he called, or her door when he knocked." Gray's eyes were troubled when they locked with Hali's turbulent gaze. "That doesn't sound good to me. You said you've met the assistant. I've seen her around but haven't talked to her. What are your opinions on her?"

Hali's stomach clenched uncomfortably. "The first time I met her I liked her," she admitted. "She wasn't adjusting to the heat well. I gave her a bag of ice for her back and talked to her for a few minutes. She seemed legitimately nice. I didn't dig too deep though."

"That could've been a deliberate move on her part," Vin argued. "She came to you while suffering. Or maybe that's simply what she wanted you to believe. If she'd spent any time watching you, she would've figured out relatively quickly that you can't stand watching anybody suffer. She might've used that to her advantage."

Hali frowned. "I happen to read people very well."

"Not when you think there's something physical working against them." Vin was matter of fact. "Your hip ailment has made you keenly aware of the limitations of others." He held up his hand when she opened her mouth to argue. "It's not a weakness, no matter what you think. You're empathetic to a fault."

"But if she used that empathy against me," Hali hedged.

"We don't know that's the case," Vin said pointedly. "Do you have a photo of this woman?" he asked Gray.

Gray nodded and touched his screen twice, bringing up a photo of Mia's sunny smile and wrinkle-free features.

"I've seen her around," Vin said grimly. "I've seen her with the shifters, in fact."

Hali's shoulders went rigid. "The shark shifters?"

"Yes." Vin's eyes were cloudy. "I saw her last night. She was on the beach near that bar where your friend works. They were beneath some trees talking."

"So, why would a tournament coordinator be talking with loan sharks?" Gray mused.

"I'm guessing she has a vested interest in making sure a certain contestant comes out on top too," Vin confirmed. "What's her relationship with Dominic Lawson?"

"I haven't seen them interact at all," Hali replied. "When I was talking to her that first time, though, she seemed to indicate Dominic was something of a tool. I'd already figured that out myself, so it didn't really come as a shock."

"Maybe that was also pointed camouflage," Vin noted. "She could've been playing you from the start, preying upon your empathy and directing the way you looked at all the other contestants."

"How can we be sure though?" Gray challenged.

"That I can't answer." Vin rubbed his forehead. "Have you talked to her since that initial conversation?" he asked Hali.

She nodded. "Yeah. I talked to her today." Her mind drifted back to the conversation, and how uncomfortable she'd felt over the course of it. "She said some weird things."

"Define weird."

"She mentioned seeing Gray and I together. She acted like she was jealous of how attentive he was, how he brushes my hair away from my face, and kisses my forehead. I thought it was odd that she'd been paying that close of attention to us."

"Yes, you two are definitely a little over the top with the touching," Vin readily agreed. "I figure you'll calm down eventually on that front. If she took the time to notice, however, there has to be a reason."

Hali could only think of one reason. "She's been watching us."

"She knows we're the ones who defused the bombs," Gray surmised. "She was probably watching the stage that day, and we didn't even realize it."

"Why try to blow up the contestants, though?" Hali demanded. "If she's really involved with the shark shifters, to the point where she wants to ensure a specific outcome, why kill her own contestant?"

"Do we even know if Dominic was scheduled to be on the stage first thing that morning?"

Hali hesitated and then shook her head. "No. I was watching the contestants that morning too. Dominic didn't arrive until the second wave of contestants. He wouldn't have been on the stage when the bombs were scheduled to go off."

Gray arched an eyebrow. "Well, I think that's your answer. She was trying to eliminate the competition."

"Because she bet on the tournament," Hali deduced. "She's looking for a payout. Does that mean Carla Hampton is dead?"

"She's either dead or being held captive," Vin replied as he finished off his drink with a flourish. "We need to get into her room. Can you arrange that?"

"I can," Gray replied as he started scrolling through his

contact list. "I'll contact Cecily. She'll have a card waiting for us at the front desk by the time we get up there."

"Then do that." Vin was grim. "The final round of the tournament is tomorrow. If this Mia person really is responsible for murder ... and setting a bomb ... then she's dangerous. She'll try to set a series of events in motion this evening. We have to get to her before that happens."

"We have to find her," Hali growled. "What if she realizes we're on to her and runs?"

"Then we'll have to deal with it. We won't know until we find her."

"Then let's find her." Gray shoved his phone in his pocket. "I want this over with, and I want it over with now."

Eighteen

Cecily came through with a room number and met the group at the door. Her gaze lingered on Vin, a question in her eyes, but when Gray announced that he was with them, she took it at face value and used the keycard to open the door.

The scent of death hit them almost immediately.

Gray extended a hand to keep Cecily back but didn't bother trying to keep Hali clear of the scene. When they flicked on the lights, there was nothing in the first bedroom. In the small living room that looked out on the Gulf, however, things were different.

"She's been stabbed," Vin said as he studied the body. The blonde's eyes were wide and sightless.

"How long has she been dead?" Hali asked. It was hard to look at the dead woman—she appeared to be in her mid-thirties at the most, although it was hard to tell given the state of the corpse—but she also couldn't look away.

"Days," Vin replied as he dropped to one knee and cocked his head to get a better look. "What day did she check in?"

"Tuesday," Cecily replied from the doorway. She didn't bother to enter the room. There was no reason to subject herself to an up-close-and-personal view. "Late in the day."

Vin did the math in his head. "I think she likely died that night."

"How come nobody mentioned the smell?" Cecily demanded.

"Because the 'do not disturb' was on the door," Gray replied. "Look at the bottom of the door too."

Hali slid her eyes in that direction, her stomach squirming when she realized there was a sheet of plastic at the bottom. It essentially served as a seal to keep the smell contained.

"What about the people in the adjacent rooms?" Hali demanded. "Wouldn't they have smelled it?"

"Eventually," Vin replied. "The air conditioning is going full throttle though. There's no humidity in this room really. The body is drying out."

"Obviously we need to wait for the coroner to confirm it, but I'm willing to bet she was stabbed by the same knife as Brian Parker," Gray said.

"Does that mean we're dealing with one killer or a team?" Hali demanded. "Brian Parker was a fit male. Sure, he wasn't overly big, but he wasn't being held back physically by age either and he would've been able to fight off a female assailant, I have to think. Mia is small."

"Yes, but is she human?" Vin queried.

Hali's initial response was a resounding yes. Then she thought about it more. "I'm not sure," she admitted after several seconds. "I didn't sense anything off about her, but that doesn't necessarily mean anything. If she's a higher paranormal than me..." She trailed off and held out her hands, helplessness washing over her.

"We need to find her," Gray said. "What room is she in?"

"Hold on." Cecily pulled out her phone and disappeared into the hallway outside the room. After almost a full minute, she returned. "She's on the sixth floor. She's got a tropical view."

"Then let's head over there." Gray strode away from the body, his gaze falling on Carla Hampton one more time. "I want to get her out of here, but I don't want to tip off Mia that we're coming for her. We need to keep this quiet until we track her down."

Cecily nodded. "I don't disagree. Let's find the killer and then deal with the damage. Shut the door."

It went against Gray's baser urges to do it, but he let the door fall shut as they exited the room. "Sixth floor next," he said.

The four of them shouldered into the elevator together. They were quiet for the two-floor trip. When they exited, there were several women dressed in party gowns giggling in the hallway. Gray smiled, because it was his natural reaction, and it was enough to draw the girls' attention.

"Do you want to come party with us?" one of them asked, slowing her pace as Gray's group kept moving.

"I appreciate the offer, but I'm busy this evening," Gray replied. "You girls have fun though."

"We're going to head down to the beach bar," the girl called out. "It's supposed to be fun. You can find us there."

"I won't be coming." Gray was firm. "I already have a girlfriend."

The young woman's gaze fell on Hali. "That's a bummer."

"Maybe for you, but not for me." Gray kept his attention moving forward as they trudged toward Mia's room. When they arrived, he pounded on the door and demanded she open up. Nobody was surprised when she didn't appear.

"I have a master," Cecily said as she handed the key to

Gray. "I think I'll stay back here though. You know, just in case."

"That's a wise idea." Gray shoved open the door once the card reader turned green. He wasn't surprised to find the room empty, however. "She's not here."

"What about her stuff?" Hali asked, pushing past him. Mia's room was small. Just two beds and a bathroom. There was no balcony or sitting room.

"It's still here." Vin gestured toward the closet. "Her clothes are hanging up. I don't think she fled. I think she's just out."

"So, where would she go?" Hali planted her hands on her hips as she scanned the room. Then it hit her. "Dominic. If we're right, she somehow has a way to give him an edge—like maybe she really does have a copy of the questions for tomorrow's round—and she could be up there quizzing him."

"It's worth a shot." Gray led the caravan out of the room and toward the elevator again. "I guess I'm going to get to use the card you provided me with," he said to Cecily, managing a half smile that didn't touch his eyes. "We'll have the element of surprise on our hands."

"No knocking?" Cecily queried.

"No knocking," Gray confirmed. "Not this time. If Dominic is mad, he can be mad. If he's entertaining someone, they'll get over it. If Mia really is in there, however, it's best to take her by surprise. We don't want to give her time to come up with a plan."

"I'm good with that." Cecily was grim as they got in the elevator to go up a single floor. "Is this going to get ugly, Gray?" she asked in a low voice.

Gray hesitated and then held out his hands. "I honestly don't know. We don't know what she is."

"But you do feel she's something," Cecily pressed.

"I think she has to be," he replied after a moment's contemplation. "We'll find out soon enough."

He used the keycard to get past the security panel that closed off the executive suite and then led the group to the penthouse door. They were quiet—it was best to take Mia by surprise after all, they'd all agreed upon that—and Gray spared Hali one glance as he prepared to let them into Dominic's room. Emotions spilled across his face as he regarded her. They ran the gamut. Ultimately, he managed a smile.

"Don't burn the place down if you start throwing around magic," he warned in a whisper, before pressing a quick kiss to her lips. When he straightened, he waved the keycard in front of the reader, and gave the heavy door a tremendous push as soon as the scanner light turned green.

He didn't call out to Dominic. He didn't offer a warning they were present. Instead, he snarled, his hands transforming into claws, as Mia hopped up from the chair she was calmly sitting in and read the situation with impassive eyes.

"Well, this doesn't seem like a friendly visit," she drawled, her eyes hopping from face to face as she slipped closer to the sliding glass doors, which were open.

"Don't!" Hali waved her hand, magic exploding, and the sliding glass doors slammed shut—and locked—within a split second.

"Neat parlor trick," Mia drawled as she glanced toward what would've been her escape route. "Should I even bother playing innocent?"

"I think we're beyond that," Gray replied. He held up a hand to still Dominic, who had missed their entrance because he was in another room. Now the trivia guru emerged from the kitchen, a glass with what looked to be some sort of cocktail inside clutched in his hand.

He looked surprised. "What's going on?" Dominic

demanded as he registered the new faces. "What are you doing here?"

"We're here for her." Gray inclined his head toward Mia, who looked more resigned than upset. "It seems she's been a bad girl."

"What do they mean?" Dominic asked Mia. He looked genuinely confused. "Is it because you've been helping me study?" When he turned back to Gray, he looked frustrated. "They're just flash cards. It's not a big deal."

Gray almost felt sorry for him. "It's a bit more extensive than that," he replied in a soft voice. "They weren't flashcards. They were the real cards from the game. She's been prepping you for the tournament with the real questions so you can beat the others."

Dominic immediately started shaking his head. "Why would she want to do that? I mean, we're together, but there's no reason to cheat to win. I'm good enough I don't need to cheat. I just need to study."

Mia's eye roll behind Dominic's back told Gray all he needed to know.

"I don't think that's actually the case," he replied. "Just out of curiosity, how long have you been together?"

"A few months." Dominic's lips curved down. "It just sort of happened. I've known Mia for two years now. A few months ago, it was like a switch went off in my brain, though. Suddenly, I saw how great she was.

"Tournament organizers can't date contestants though," he continued. "It's one of the rules. We had to keep it quiet. That's why I kept mentioning other women when I talked to you. It was a show, so nobody would find out. I'm really not that bad. You won't tell anybody, will you? Carla won't understand."

"Carla is dead," Gray replied, his gaze on Mia. She didn't

flinch. She didn't look surprised by the news. She merely smirked. "Your girlfriend killed her," he added.

"That's ridiculous," Dominic sputtered, his eyes flashing dark. "She would never do anything of the sort."

"Well, she did." Gray ran his tongue over his teeth. The situation remained fluid. They had Mia outnumbered, but they still didn't know what they were dealing with. It was a tense situation. "I thought you were a ladies' man. You picked up a woman the first night you were here."

Dominic chuckled. "Actually, I didn't. I stayed in my room all night like a good boy. I didn't even see Mia that night because she had a work meeting go late. I only told you that I picked up a woman at the bar because I wanted to keep the Dominic Lawson mystique alive." He puffed out his chest.

"Because you actually love her," he surmised.

"Look, I'm as surprised as anybody that it happened," Dominic said. "I never thought I was in it for the big L. I am though. I'm happy. Just because she's helping me study, that doesn't mean we're cheating though. We can have a relationship that's separate from the tournament. I promise."

Gray blinked twice and then switched his gaze back to Mia. "Do you want to be the one to tell him, or should I?"

"It doesn't matter now, does it?" Mia spat. "You're going to ruin tomorrow no matter what."

"I'm pretty sure you ruined the finale when you killed two people," Gray shot back.

"Oh, listen to you." She made a clucking sound with her tongue before focusing on Hali. "I knew I let too much slip today when I was talking to you. I thought I still had time though. I guess that's on me for underestimating you. I won't do that again."

"What are you even talking about?" Dominic demanded. "Why are you pretending Mia is responsible for any of this?"

"Because I am," Mia replied softly. She was apparently

over hiding if the look on her face signified anything. "I killed Brian Parker. I killed Carla Hampton too."

Dominic was flabbergasted. "Why?"

"Because I needed you to win."

"I'm guessing she's been helping you study for a long time," Gray replied. "Before, she managed to pull it off without tipping anybody off. This time, the purse was bigger though."

"She's been stealing the questions from the guy who handled the cards," Hali explained. "Brian Parker may have locked the questions in the safe, but Mia had access to that safe. I'm guessing Brian figured that out because Dominic kept winning at specific tournaments, and that's why he died."

"He should've kept his mouth shut," Mia replied evenly. "I offered him a cut of my take, but he wouldn't listen."

"Are you being serious?" Dominic's voice took on an edge as he turned to face Mia. "Are you telling me you were betting on me?"

"Oh, look at you." Mia's lips quirked. "You actually look sad. We both got something out of this arrangement."

"But I loved you," Dominic whined. "I thought we were going to be a super couple, like they're a super couple." He waved at Hali and Gray. "That's what I wanted."

"You're a cupid, show a little pride," Mia shot back. "You're not supposed to be picturing yourself as the leading man in a Hallmark movie. If you're going to be on a television show, at least make it a soap opera."

Dominic worked his jaw. When he flicked his eyes back to Gray, there was genuine hurt there. "I don't understand."

"I know." Gray felt sorry for the man, but there was very little he could do for him. "She's been betting on your performance. She's working with the local loan sharks."

"Who are literal sharks," Hali added because she couldn't help herself.

"Shark shifters," Gray corrected. "They're here. They're trying to influence others to bet against you. They would only do that if they thought you were a sure thing. I'm willing to bet Mia has been feeding information to the betting agents in every stop you guys have made since getting together. That would give her more favorable odds when she won."

Mia looked smug. "It worked like a charm too. I have quite the nest egg built up."

"You're not going to get to use it," Hali countered. "It was all a waste."

"Is that so?" Mia didn't look convinced. "How do you figure that?"

"We're not just going to let you get away with this," Gray replied. "You've killed two people. We can't just ignore that."

"You could," Mia countered. "I could pay you to ignore it."

"Some things are more important than money," Gray countered. "I think you need to walk this way. Extend your hands as you're doing it." He reached to the back of his belt and retrieved a pair of handcuffs. They were magical. He used them in his line of work all the time. "We don't want this to get ugly when it doesn't have to."

Flames ignited in the depths of Mia's eyes at the words. Actual flames, and that's when the final piece of the puzzle slid into place for Hali.

"You're a fire elemental." It wasn't a question. She simply knew.

"Does it matter?" Mia demanded.

"It just makes sense," Hali replied. "Your fire would've appealed to his air elements." She angled her head toward Dominic. "He would've had no choice but to be attracted to you."

"It worked out well," Mia agreed. "Now it's done though, and I'm really not happy. I wanted that big win tomorrow.

Dominic was going to get his purse, and I was going to win big on my bet. You're ruining everything."

"Do you want me to say we're sorry about that?" Gray demanded. "Because we're not. You're the one killing people."

"Oh, whine, whine, whine." Mia made an exaggerated face. "You can't stop me. If you try, I'll burn down this entire hotel and still make my escape. If you want to keep this place intact, then you'll let me go." She gestured toward the closed sliding glass doors.

"Yeah, that's not happening," Gray declared. "You're going into custody. We're not letting you go."

"Fine." Mia sounded as if she didn't have a care in the world. "Let's do it the hard way." Her hands caught fire—literally—as she raised them. Before she could unleash the torrent, however, she found herself caught.

Vin had moved so fast she didn't even register he was in the room. He had her by the throat when she managed her first blink. Hali was fast in his wake. She grabbed Mia's hands and exerted her own magic to extinguish the flames.

It was only then that Mia registered she was in real trouble. "What are you doing?" she demanded, her voice going shrill. "What do you think you're doing?"

"Putting an end to this before it gets out of hand," Gray replied. He was grim as he snapped the handcuffs around her wrists. "We want you contained before the police come for you, so you should know that these handcuffs are cursed. If you try to use your magic while they're on you, it will ricochet back and hurt you."

Mia was obviously dubious because she tried throwing out a blast of fire despite his warning. Within an instant, her eyebrows had been singed off, and she looked like some weird modeling mishap as she blinked and made a guttural sound deep in her throat.

"There it is," Gray said as he briefly shut his eyes. "That's a lovely smell. There's nothing better than the scent of burnt hair." He made a gagging noise.

"It's terrible," Vin agreed, releasing his hold on her neck. He almost looked disappointed that he hadn't been allowed to shed some blood. "I might gag it's so bad."

"I didn't think vampires had a gag reflex," Hali said. "Didn't you once tell me that?"

"No, I said I had an iron constitution. There's a difference."

"Whatever." Hali was solemn as she stared into Mia's furious eyes. It was obvious that the fire elemental was looking for a way out. There was nothing there for her to grab onto though. Her entire world had been wiped away in a matter of seconds. "I bet you're wishing you'd picked another path to follow."

"Oh, I'm not done yet." Mia's voice was oily and threatening. "I'm nowhere near done."

"I think that just proves how delusional you really are," Gray shot back. His eyes moved to Dominic, who had flopped onto the couch and seemed to be staring into nothing. "Maybe I should stay here for a bit," he suggested to Hali. "You know, just for a spot of conversation."

Hali's heart expanded in size. Gray was a good man, and that was almost always on display. Tonight, even though he wasn't particularly fond of Dominic, he recognized the trivia guru was spiraling. He didn't want to leave him alone under those circumstances.

"I get it," Hali promised. "Vin can help us deliver Mia to Andrew. You stay here as long as you need."

"It won't be long," Gray promised. "Make sure she gets back to the villa safely, huh?" he prodded Vin.

"I will." The vampire showed off his teeth as he smiled. "Per usual, it was a pleasure doing business with you."

"Yeah, I don't know if I would phrase it like that. Nobody lost their life tonight though. I'm going to take it as a win."

"That's exactly how you should take it. You did well."

"*We* did well," Gray corrected, winking at Hali. "I won't be long. Don't go to bed without me."

"I'll be waiting," she promised as she directed Mia toward the door. "I'll see you soon."

"You will, and I can't wait."

NINETEEN

Dominic ended up disqualifying himself from the trivia final round. It didn't even take much prodding on Gray's part to make it happen. That meant there were only four people in the last round battling it out, and even though Lana was apparently thrown by the change, she was all smiles when she took the stage.

"What do you think?" Gray asked from his normal stool. His eyes were on Hali instead of Lana. They'd sweated through a long night and enjoyed a cuddly morning. She remained an enigma, however.

"I think she has a good shot," Hali replied. The bar was packed with people watching the finale, and she had extra workers on to cover both the patio and the beach. That meant she could take time out to chat with Gray over an iced tea. "What about you?"

Gray shrugged as he accepted the glass she handed him. "I'm good. I got paid by Franklin already. Actually, the check was handed over by Cecily, and I deposited it immediately."

"Good idea." Hali grinned. "Did you give her back the contract for the succession clause?"

"I did. She said everything was good and it was being officially filed, whatever that means. She'll have a receipt for you tomorrow."

Hali's smile widened. "I didn't get a chance to properly thank you for what you did," she started.

"I don't need to be thanked."

"I'm talking." She rested her hand on his forearm and pinned him with a pointed look. "You took this job because of me, and I'm grateful. You didn't have to negotiate on my behalf, but you did because you wanted me to be protected. I can't ever thank you enough for that."

He waited to make sure she was finished. "Can I talk now?" he asked finally.

She nodded.

"Good. I want you protected because I care about you. Even if something terrible were to happen and we were to somehow split apart—and I don't want that ever—I wouldn't be able to live with the notion of you not being protected. What I did wasn't special. It was a necessity."

She blinked twice, as if holding off tears, and then nodded. "I still appreciate it."

"That's nice." He moved his hand on top of hers. "You can reward me later."

"You're spending the night again?" Hali couldn't hide her delight.

"Baby, wild shark shifters couldn't drag me away." He leaned in for a kiss, savored her for a moment, and then forced himself to pull back. Now wasn't the time to get romantic. There were far too many people around. "I have a report, if you're interested."

"Absolutely." She waved a hand in front of her face, her cheeks flushed. "It will do me good to focus on something other than you for a little bit."

"I like being your focus." He winked and then sobered.

"Andrew is arranging for Mia to be transferred to a different jail. It's a paranormal one. They have her locked up in a special cell right now, but it's one of those things where only a handful of people in the department even know about magic. There's not enough security to ensure she won't escape, so she's being moved."

Hali cocked her head to the side, considering, and then nodded. "I guess that makes sense. What will happen to her?"

"Well, the news stories will be skewed to avoid the magical angle. Her trial won't be open to the public. They'll come up with a cover, like they always do. When she's locked away, though, there will never be a chance of her getting out again. As a fire elemental, she's always going to have to be secured in a specific way."

"I don't happen to think she deserves a chance to get out," Hali admitted. "She killed two people. It wasn't in a fit of rage either. She didn't momentarily lose her mind. It was planned."

"She's admitted that Brian Parker figured out what was going on," Gray supplied. "He tried to blackmail her. She'd been cheating for months, stealing the cards and helping Dominic 'study' without telling him what her true motivation was." He used the appropriate air quotes.

"Brian figured it out because Mia wasn't being chill when spending the money," he continued. "He started watching her, even filmed her breaking into a hotel safe in Texas. She paid him once, but she refused to pay him again. He made the mistake of meeting her on the beach, and she ended him."

"And where does Carla play into all this?" Hali queried. Nothing Gray had said so far surprised her.

"She saw Mia and Brian on the beach together. Mia wasn't actually planning on killing Brian. She had the knife on her just in case, but she hoped to talk him down. She just wanted to make it through this tournament, and then she was going to take off with her winnings."

"She couldn't do that when Brian started threatening her," Hali surmised. "That makes sense. Then, because she knew Carla had seen them together and didn't want her sharing the information with the police, she took out Carla too."

"She seemed genuinely elated that Carla had gone so long without being discovered," Gray confirmed. "She's clearly a sociopath."

"Now she's the one who will spend the rest of her life in prison," Hali mused. "It seems fair."

"It does."

"What about Rip and Finn?"

Gray took a sip of his iced tea before answering. "They knew she'd placed a big bet, and on their guy. They claim that they had no idea Dominic was being provided with the answers ahead of time."

"Do you believe them?"

"No." Gray emphatically shook his head. "Not even a little. The thing is, I don't believe they knew about the murders. I mean ... they did, but they had no idea Mia was the one carrying them out. Truth be told, this is the worst thing that could ever happen to them. Dominic pulling out means they're going to lose all the money that they put on him. The thing is, they get to keep all the money Mia put on him. There's no way to claim it from them."

"Oh." Realization dawned on Hali. "So, they came out ahead after all?"

"A lot of people put money on Dominic. They'll have to pay out on some of the bets given who wins, but they lost their own money to themselves. They also got all the money that was paid in on Dominic. At worst, they've admitted they're going to break even. That's not the outcome they wanted, but it could've been worse."

"What's their best-case scenario?" Hali queried.

"If Lana wins, they come out way ahead. Enough so they can help their father out of debt on that resort."

"Interesting," Hali mused, her eyes darting to the stage. The contest was in full swing now, and in an hour, a victor would be declared.

"Now you're torn, right?" Gray prodded. "You don't want Lana to win because it means Rip and Finn will win too."

"Actually, that's not what I was thinking," Hali replied. "I want Lana to win. It's what's best for her. If they win too, I don't care. I want what's best for my friend."

"That's because you're amazing." He leaned in and nuzzled his nose against her cheek, grinning when she made a groaning noise. When he pulled back, he was rueful. "How late are you going to be open tonight?"

"Not late. The contest is over in an hour. I figure the guests will keep drinking for two hours after that. I'm planning on shutting down at five o'clock. Why?"

"Because I want to spend some time with you."

"Doing what?" Hali's smile was playful.

"I thought we could have a picnic on the beach."

She snorted. "The last time we did that, you complained about sand in your boxer shorts."

"And yet it's still worth it."

Her heart, she was mortified to realize, had gone to mush. "How about we compromise?" she countered. "Why don't we go out for a nice dinner? I'll buy. I want some seafood."

"The place down on the beach you love so much?"

She nodded. "I want crab legs."

"There's nothing I love more than watching you try to wash your hands with a wet-nap when you've got Cajun seasoning flecks spread from your hands to your elbows," he teased.

Hali pretended he hadn't spoken. "Then, when we're finished with dinner, we can take a walk on the beach," she continued. "I'll even let you carry me if my hip becomes an issue, and I won't utter a single complaint."

He tugged the strand of hair that had come loose from her bun behind her ear. He still wanted to talk to her about surgery ... and maybe about a shaman. It wasn't time yet though. His job was to be there for her. Her job was to make that decision on her own when she was ready.

"I think that sounds like exactly how I want to spend my evening," he said in a husky voice.

"Good." She beamed at him. "Let's spend the early part of the afternoon rooting for Lana and getting through the heavy stuff. Then we'll take the rest of the day for ourselves."

"I'm right there for all of that."

They held hands as they watched the tournament, and when Lana won, they clapped louder than anybody else. Sure, life wasn't perfect, but things could be a whole lot worse.

Of course, with the dark merrow circling and preparing to make a move, there was no telling when the "worse" would be upon them.

Made in the USA
Middletown, DE
08 June 2023